Frag Box

Books by Richard A. Thompson

The Herman Jackson Mysteries
Fiddle Game
Frag Box

Other Novels
Big Wheat

Frag Box

A Herman Jackson Mystery

Richard A. Thompson

Poisoned Pen Press

Poisoned
Pen
Press

Poisoned Pen Press
6962 E. First Ave., Ste. 103
Scottsdale, AZ 85251
www.poisonedpenpress.com
info@poisonedpenpress.com

Printed in the United States of America

This one is for Helen.

Acknowledgments

The creative process never occurs in a vacuum. I am enormously indebted to the following people for their unstinting help with this project:

Jim Woodward, who fleshed out the landscape of 1960s Detroit for me;

Tate Halverson, who kept my descriptions of Vietnam-era Army organization accurate;

My long-suffering writing buddies, Peter Farley and Ingrid Trausch, who gave me priceless ongoing critical analysis and moral support;

And of course, Margaret Yang, my indispensable beta reader and soul mate.

As usual, my humble thanks are quite inadequate.

frag. [1] A fragmentation grenade. [2] To explode a fragmentation grenade. [3] To kill or wound one's superior officer, from the fact that a fragmentation grenade was often the weapon of choice.

Paul Dickson,
War Slang: American Fighting Words and Phrases from the Civil War to the War in Iraq, Second Edition
Potomac Books, Inc. (formerly Brassey's, Inc., XXXX)

frag pot. A place for collecting money to induce somebody to kill an officer; from the fact that the preferred container was often a helmet, or "pot."

Common G.I. slang, Vietnam War

frag box. The same as above, only in civilian life.

Charles Victor, veteran

Prologue

Eveleth, Minnesota
Early March, 1968

It was twelve degrees below zero when he got off the bus. He still had fifteen miles to go, but Eveleth was the end of the line, as far north as the Greyhound would take him. He would have to hitch hike the rest of the way to the town of Mountain Iron, where his parents had a tiny house. Neither the town nor the house nor the parents were much to come home to, but they were what he had.

After four years in the service, three of them in Vietnam, he had finally had enough. The Army had dangled a big wad of money and some stripes in front of him, but this time, he didn't bite. He mustered out and went back to the World.

His class A uniform and greatcoat were no match for the cold, and he had nothing to cover his hands or ears. He decided to get a few shots of antifreeze before starting the rest of his trip, and he walked the two blocks to Main Street, weaving between mountains of shoveled snow that towered above his head.

Downtown, upstairs over an appliance store, there was a VFW bar. He assumed he would be welcomed there. With his uniform and his ribbons, he might get a freebie or two, or even a ride home. Who knew?

At the side of the appliance store, he opened a frosted-over glass door, kicked the snow off his polished jump boots, and climbed the stairs.

Upstairs was a workingman's bar, with a small hardwood dance floor that hadn't been varnished in thirty years and cheap paneling on the walls, adorned with stuffed moose and deer heads and phony looking lacquered fish. Beams of feeble late afternoon light from a few narrow windows pierced the smoke and dust and illuminated a big American flag on a floor standard and some dingy patriotic bunting over the bar. Under the moose head, a movie poster of Jane Fonda in her sex-kitten role from *Barbarella* had obviously been used as a dartboard, with the moose also getting his share of random punctures. The tables and chairs were all stacked and pushed against the outside wall, but that didn't matter, because the seven or eight regular patrons all sat at the bar.

They looked interchangeable: dumpy-looking retired or out-of-work men in dirty baseball caps, plaid shirts, and Osh Kosh work pants held up by wide suspenders. Their Chippewa or Red Wing boots rested on the brass rail, showing rubber soles worn to banana-shaped profiles. They also wore expressions of well-practiced boredom, and they hunched low over the bar, nursing flat beers, trying to keep an all-day buzz going on a scanty mining pension or an unemployment check. They did not chat. The bartender was younger, though definitely not young, and he wore black slacks and a white shirt with a crumpled clip-on bow tie.

Near the door was a jukebox with selections by such worthies as Whoopee John, Frankie Yankovik, and The Six Fat Dutchmen, but it wasn't playing. This was not a place for music. Everything here was yesterday, elsewhere, and too bad.

All eyes turned when the young sergeant came in with a cloud of frigid air. He took off his greatcoat and hung it on a peg, dumping his duffle on the floor nearby. Most of the regulars turned back to stare into their beers, but some of them smirked and exchanged knowing looks.

"Anybody looking to buy some cookies?" said one of the smirkers. "I think the Girl Scouts just came in."

The soldier ignored him and took a stool near the center of the bar.

"Beer and a bump," he said.

The bartender made no move to get him anything.

"You a member?"

He couldn't believe what he was hearing. He spread his arms wide, to display his chest full of ribbons, including a purple heart with a bronze V in the proper position of honor, top row, inside.

"Well," he said, "I am damn sure a veteran, and of the foreign-ist goddamn war the politicians ever made. What else you gotta have?"

"This place is for members only," said the bartender, now folding his arms and tilting his chin up aggressively.

"Aah, give the kid a drink," said a voice from the end of the bar.

"Who the hell asked you?"

"He wears the uniform, he's entitled."

"Not if he ain't a member. He ain't entitled to diddly shit." That brought a chorus of muttered agreements from up and down the bar.

"That's bullshit, and you know it," said the lone dissenter on the end, a stumpy, bowlegged troll with a barrel chest and a full white beard. He detached himself from his stool and came over, his hand extended.

"Luther Johnson," he said. "I was with the Seabees in Burma."

"He was with the Salvation Army in Bumfuck, is where he was," said another regular. "He has a half a beer, he gets all confused."

"No, he don't. The two are the same thing."

"Throw the both of them out, Mack."

"Fucking-ay. We don't need their kind here."

"Charlie Victor," said the soldier, taking the hand. That brought a whoop from the others.

"He not only couldn't beat the enemy, he took their name!"

Johnson stood his ground. "Can that shit," he said. "I'm a paid up member, and Charlie here is my guest. Pour him a drink."

"You ain't paid your tab in two weeks, Luther," said the bartender, though now he moved to get a glass from the counter behind the bar.

"Well, it ain't the end of the month, is it? I ever stiff you on it?"

"Just don't be calling yourself paid up, is all I'm saying."

"Listen, mister civilian barhop, you can—"

"How much is his tab?" said Victor.

"What do you care?"

"How much?"

"I dunno without looking it up. Twenty, maybe twenty-two or three bucks. Mind your own business, soldier boy."

The soldier reached into his wallet and dug out a twenty and a five and slapped them on the bar top.

"My friend Luther is all paid up, okay? Now give us both a drink."

"I can pay my own way, kid."

"No shit. And I can fight my own battles."

"Really?" The voice belonged to somebody slightly younger and a lot bigger than Johnson, though still cut from the same common mold. He slid off his stool and came up behind them, doing his best to look imposing despite a sagging beer belly and unfocused eyes.

"Seems to me all you candy-ass, druggie Viet Conga boys know how to do is whine, get high, and lose."

Somewhere in a primitive part of Victor's brain, old wheels began to turn, mixing dark impulses into explosive slurry, begging him to add a detonating spark. But he ignored it with a force of pure will, also ignored the fat, belligerent drunk.

"Are we square now, or what?" he said to the bartender.

The bartender didn't answer, but he poured a shot of rye and slammed it down on the bar, deliberately slopping some over the side. Then he drew two beers and put them on the bar top as well. After he had scooped up the money and stuffed it in the till, he walked back to where the soldier was throwing back the shot and pointedly spat into his beer. The cogs turned a notch farther and the juices started to approach critical mass.

"Just exactly what is your problem?" said Victor as calmly as he could.

"His problem's same as our problem," said Beer Belly, now coming close enough to poke him in the arm. "His problem is that we won our war. We didn't protest and we didn't run off to Canada and we didn't get high on dope and badmouth our country. We didn't fuck up."

"What makes you think I did?"

"Well you damn sure ain't won, have you?" The bartender again, and Victor turned back to stare into his eyes.

"And just exactly which war did you win, Mr. Bowtie?"

"Well, I, um—"

"He don't have to have been in any war to respect the guys who was. He knows how to act. But you phony jungle heroes with your pussy berets don't even know how to do that. You screw around and you keep this damn war going, and pretty soon some real Americans are going to have to go over there and die."

"Like his precious kid," said Johnson.

"What about it? My kid is college material, is what he is. His hockey coach pret' near said so. This asshole here's nothing but mine slag. That's probably why he got drafted; they always take the trash first. And if he couldn't finish the job, he shoun't a come back."

The final bit of machinery clicked. To Victor's surprise, though, the wave of rage that flooded through him was cold, quiet, and supremely controlled. And he knew exactly what he was going to do with it.

"You know what's wrong with war?" said Victor. "I mean, three tours in-country and two purple hearts, and I didn't figure it out until just now. Do you know?"

"Easy, man," said Johnson. "Maybe you should—"

"Oh, now we're gonna get the peace and love speech." Beer Belly turned sideways to play to the rest of the regulars, but before he could say another word, Victor took the glass with beer and spit and smashed it against the side of the man's head. Foam and blood ran down his pasty face, obscuring one smashed eye. The other eye bulged, matching the astonished "o" of the mouth below it. The man howled but didn't go down, so Victor gave him a solid jab to the solar plexus, dropping him in a blubbering heap.

Behind him, Victor heard Johnson say, "Whatever you're reaching for under that bar, Mack, it better be made out of chocolate, 'cause I think you're about to eat it."

Victor whirled around to see the bartender pull a sawed-off baseball bat from under the bar. But before he could do anything with it, Johnson pounded the man's forearm with the side of his fist, pinning the arm to the bar top. The hand went limp. Victor snatched the bat and shoved the end of it into the man's mouth, grabbing a fistful of greasy hair with his other hand, preventing him from backing away.

"What's wrong with war," he said, staring intently into the bartender's eyes, "is that the wrong people always die."

Johnson said something he didn't hear, and the bartender tried to say something but couldn't. Victor shoved the bat down his throat, as hard and as far as he could. He felt things tear and break and squish, and he gave himself over utterly to the delicious black rage that flooded his brain.

Up and down the bar, nobody else moved. No beers were drunk and nobody spoke as they waited in frozen terror to see what the crazy Vietnam vet would do next.

The lunatic went around behind the bar, where the bartender now lay on the floor, convulsing and making choking, gurgling sounds. Victor ignored him. He slammed two handfuls of shot glasses up on the bar and poured them full from two bottles of liquor he picked up at random, one in each hand. He sent the glasses sliding up and down the bar, distributing them, then continued to pour. He doused liquor on the bodies on the floor and flooded the bar top.

"Drinks all around," he said. "On the house." In the background, he saw Johnson go over to the pay phone on the wall and rip out the receiver cord.

"Drink, you sonsabitches," he screamed, "or I swear I'll kill every fucking one of you!"

They drank.

Over by the phone, Johnson made a gesture toward the door.

"Time we got out of here, kid."

He nodded, held up a finger in a gesture that said "just one minute." Then he took out his Zippo lighter and calmly lit the puddles of booze.

‹›‹›‹›

What the rest of the regulars said or did after that, he would never know. Nor did he know what else, if anything, he did to them. The next conscious memory he had was of himself and Johnson running over brittle-crusted snow to jump on an ore train that was laboring up a grade on the edge of town. Twenty miles later, just outside the Erie Mining plant, they swapped it for a ride on a trainload of processed taconite pellets, headed for the dockyards at Duluth. It was blackest night by then, and the temperature seemed to drop almost as fast as the train speeded up. They huddled on the machinery platform at one end of a big hopper car, holding onto the framework with arms looped around steel bars. Neither of them had gloves, and they didn't dare grab the frigid metal with their bare hands. Somewhere between Hoyt Lakes and Duluth, Luther Johnson froze to death.

"So it's true in the World, too," said Victor. "Always the wrong ones who get killed."

He jumped off the train in West Duluth, dumped his uniform, except for the boots and fatigue jacket, in a dumpster at a truck stop, and started hitchhiking. South. In a Catholic church across the street from a gas station in Cloquet, he stopped long enough to light two candles, one for Luther Johnson and one for himself. He was not a Catholic, but it seemed like the right thing to do. Then he continued heading south.

He never made it back to Mountain Iron, to the father who had once told him to go off to war. He settled in St. Paul, finally, sometimes living on the street, sometimes with a former hooker in Lowertown, in the wino district.

"It's always the wrong ones get killed," he told her, when one of their fellow winos died from drinking antifreeze.

"Well, why don't you quit your whining and do something about it?"

So he did.

Blood Game

It was a day for pocket billiards, snow, and death. The snow came in the late afternoon, in fat, globular flakes that swirled in the eddies of the urban canyons, stuck to the rough brick of old buildings, and covered the streets in a layer of slush for cars to splash onto pedestrians. On the windows of Lefty's Pool Hall and Saloon in downtown St. Paul, they dribbled down the dirty glass and made mushy heaps on the sills, leaving crooked, wet trails behind them.

I was inside Lefty's at the time, shooting eight ball with Wide Track Wilkie. And while the hapless man on the street below was lost in a world of pain and despair, we were lost in the click of the balls and the smell of smoke and stale beer and the electric tension of money being put in harm's way.

Lefty's is an old-fashioned pool hall, a walkup flight above a not-quite-downtown street, with high ceilings and lazy Bombay fans and green-shaded hanging lamps. It has pool tables with real leather pockets and no coin slots, and snooker and billiards tables, too. And it has high, multi-paned windows. You have to stand on tiptoe to see anything out of them except the sky. It's an easy world to get lost in.

Wilkie likes eight ball, because it's slow and it gives him a lot of time to hustle side bets. I like it because it lets me get more mileage out of finesse than power, which means I can beat him sometimes. At snooker, I almost always can. At nine ball, never.

He can sink the money ball on the break one time out of every six, and those are odds that I can't ignore. And I am nothing if not a believer in odds. So for our separate reasons, we agreed to play straight eight.

Back about a hundred years ago, in the shiny chrome city of Detroit, I worked for my Uncle Fred, a bookie and numbers man and the smartest handicapper I've ever known. He taught me that the secret to all of life is nothing more than being able to figure the correct odds. That, and knowing who the house is and always betting with it.

After he went upstate for the second time, I used his money to start a bail bond business, which I figured was as house as you can get. And I was doing okay, with more cash flow than any of Fred's games produced and none of the risk. But I forgot his second secret to life, which is never to be your own customer. I foolishly used my office to recruit some talent for a caper that went not at all well, and I wound up having to flee The Motor City for good. I kept my old name, Herman Jackson, since it's a common enough one, but I changed everything else. I started a new bail bond business and a new life in St. Paul. It's the capital of Minnesota, of course, and I suppose that makes it important, but I always think of it as an uneventful old shoe of a city, which was exactly what I wanted.

Now I spend my days quietly, playing low stakes pool in Lefty's and writing get-out-of-jail cards for small-time losers too stupid to stay there. I bet only the smart odds, and I spend a lot of time looking over my shoulder.

Sooner or later, I suppose, that had to change.

That afternoon, the odds didn't seem to matter. I was on a roll, and I had just dropped the seven ball with a long-green shot as soft and subtle as destiny's whisper, leaving the old timers in the place thumping the butts of their cues on the floor in muffled applause.

"Nice," said Wilkie.

"I thought so," I said.

"Yeah," he said, rocking on his heels and making the floor groan in the process. "Slicker than snot on a doorknob. It ought to make you feel so good, Herman my man, you forgive yourself in advance for missing the next one, which you are definitely going to do."

"You wish."

"I know. Look it over, man."

I looked. I had only the solid-colored black eight ball, the money ball, left to shoot, while Wilkie still had three striped balls on the table. But the eight was backed up in a corner, frozen against the end rail and totally hidden by the thirteen. In the other direction, down the table, there wasn't enough English in a whole bottle of Beefeater's to let me miss the nine and fifteen and do a two-cushion double around the far corner. I could do a deliberate scratch, without touching the eight, and stay in the game, but that would give Wilkie another turn at shooting, which was never a very good idea. For reasons I will never fathom, I decided to go down with style.

"Massé," I said.

"You can't be serious."

"Have you ever known me otherwise?"

"A hundred bucks says you can't make it."

I looked over the setup again. He was right; I couldn't make it.

"A hundred to my twenty," I said.

"Five to one? Are you nuts? I wouldn't give my sweet old grandma five to one."

"If I had your grandma shooting for me, I'd give you three to five. But you're so damn sure I can't do it, you ought to be willing to be a little sporting."

"Hey, I am a little sporting. I promise not to bounce on the floor while you're setting up to miss. Five to three, then; my hundred to your sixty."

"You bounce on the floor, and all bets are off." Wilkie is over four hundred pounds on the hoof. When his stomach rumbles, so does the earth around him.

"I said I wouldn't, didn't I?"

I looked at the shot again and made a few practice strokes. It really was a terrible setup. A massé is a bizarre shot where you actually stroke the cue ball vertically, as if you were trying to drive it straight down into the table. But you hit it off center, and it goes drunkenly spinning off, waltzing around the ball you have to avoid and back to the one you want to hit. Sometimes. It's never all that easy to do, let alone with exact control. And with the eight ball frozen against the cushion, this one had to be perfect. But for any event in the entire universe, there are odds. And if the odds are right, you have to play. That's another secret of life, which my uncle Fred did not teach me. "Four to one," I said, "nonnegotiable."

"Remind me never to buy a used car from you. All right, against my better judgment, your lousy twenty-five bucks to my hundred."

"I've only got twenty on me, Wide. I told you that up front." And truth to tell, I shouldn't even be risking that. My cash flow situation just then was a disaster.

Wilkie groaned. "I'll carry you, Mr. High Roller."

"Nope." I shook my head while he looked as if he were about to blow a gasket somewhere in his vital machinery. "I never play for what I haven't got. You know that."

"Listen, Superchicken, if you—"

"Call the cops!"

All heads turned to a shapeless character in a dirty parka and watch cap, charging in the main door and screaming at Lefty, who was at his usual spot behind the bar.

"They killed a man out there!"

"Who did?" said Lefty.

"The hell difference does it make, who? Call the cops, will you? And gimmie a beer. And a shot, while you're at it."

Part of the crowd went to the windows and gave out a bunch of noises like, "awgeez," and "willya lookathat?" The rest of them headed for the door. I leaned toward a window.

"Screw that," said Wilkie. "Take the damn shot."

"Who's dead?" I said, looking over the setup with the eight again. It didn't get any better with further study.

"Looks like old Charlie Vee," said one of the voices at the window.

"Oh, shit," I said, and my shoulders sagged. "You sure?" I suddenly had a sinking sensation in my stomach and no interest in the game at all.

"Hard to tell for sure from here," said the voice. "He's messed up awful bad."

I put down the cue stick and headed for the door, leaving Wilkie to fume about the bet. The first shouts of anger and denial inside my own head were already drowning him out.

I didn't know if Lefty had made the phone call yet or not. When I passed him, he was pouring the drinks for the bearer of ill tidings.

"Friend of yours?" said Lefty. "The dead guy, I mean?"

"Customer," I said. At least, that was the short version.

"Always a bitch, losing a good customer."

I didn't bother to stop and explain it to him.

I don't generally look out the windows of Lefty's once in five years, but if I had done so ten minutes earlier on that day, I'd have seen it. I'd have seen them back him up against the wall and punch him in the chest and stomach until he gushed blood from his mouth and the strength went out of his legs and he sagged down against the bricks. I'd have seen when they pushed him all the way down, until he was flat on his back, and one of them stood on his chest while another one finished the job with a heavy boot. And when they spilled whatever was left of his soul onto the cold concrete, along with the addictions and nightmares he carried from the jungles of a distant, dirty war, I might have screamed. I might have. The sky was dim and gray at the time, but it was still daylight. I could have seen it all, and I could have screamed for him.

And I should have.

It makes absolutely no sense and does no good to say so, but I know I should have.

<><><>

The wet, wind-driven flakes hit me in the face and insinuated themselves inside my open collar and up my shirt cuffs, reminding me that I had run out without a coat.

Across the street, there were a dozen or more spectators ahead of me, clustered in a semicircle about ten feet back from the body on the sidewalk. Gawkers, drawn irresistibly to the sight of violent death but still wanting to keep a certain sterile distance between it and themselves. From somewhere far away, I could hear the first sirens. I pushed through the crowd and had a look, instantly regretting it. The guy at the window had not been exaggerating about how messed up the dead man was.

The face was a deflated soccer ball, smeared with blood and draped in overlong gray hair. And the body shape was masked by the countless layers of old clothes that street people collect. At first glance, it could have been anybody. But there, unmistakably, was the threadbare khaki fatigue jacket with the faded sergeant stripes and the frayed Air Cav shoulder patch. There, also, were the thick-soled work boots, their brown leather daubed endlessly with black shoe polish, to try to make them look like combat boots, because Charlie couldn't get any real combat boots at the free store on West Seventh Street. And there were the big, once powerful hands, now cruelly deformed by arthritis, with a blue tattoo of a coiled cobra on the back of the right one. I knew all that well enough, and a good bit more. It was Charlie, all right. In some ways, he was still a complete mystery to me, but I knew him when I saw him, even in this sorry state.

Charles Victor was his real name, and yes, he did once have to go to Vietnam with that most unfortunate of handles. What they called him over there, I didn't know, but I imagined that he must have had to be one hell of a soldier, just to keep from being shot by his own people. He had a lot of stories, but who knew how many of them were true?

Whatever he had really done, he never got over it. I didn't know if he fit the orthodox definition of post-traumatic stress syndrome, but for my money, he could have been a poster child for it. In Southeast Asia, the war was over decades ago. People go there as tourists now. The war in Charlie's soul went on every day, and no sane person would go there, ever. He left the jungle, but it never left him. It was always sitting on his shoulder like a dark, leathery gargoyle, waiting to trip him into quiet madness and horror. If he was violent, I never saw it, but I did see times when he just wasn't present in the real world at all. Whether for that reason or others, he never held a regular job or had a home or a woman or wanted anything from life but anonymity and oblivion. And he finally got both of them, but as usual with him, he paid way too much.

But then, there's a lot of that going around. By rights, I shouldn't have cared. What was he to me, after all? A customer, and not a very big one at that. But there was another link there, not so easy to put a name on. Sometimes I had the feeling that his story, if I knew it well enough, would also turn out to be my own. And as with my own, I knew I hadn't heard it all yet. For the moment, though, I felt sick. And at least part of that sickness was called guilt.

Footprints

"What about you? You see anything?" It was a challenge, not a question. The cop throwing it at me was fortyish, red-faced, big, and belligerent. His expression made it clear that I had damn well better have seen something, if I knew what was good for me. Otherwise, my presence on the street was an insult to the universe in general and him in particular.

"I just got here," I said, shaking my head.

"Yeah? Well, just get someplace else. The thing I do not need around here right now, is I do not need any more goddamn rubbernecks."

He had a point. So far, he was the only police presence at a scene that was drawing a crowd faster than the free bar at an Irish wake. If there had been any useful evidence in the fresh snow, the mob had already obliterated it or stuffed it in their pockets for souvenirs. Not good.

Down near the end of the block, there were still a few sets of distinct footprints, but even as we watched, a big, square-shouldered kid in a black nylon wind breaker and a stocking cap came around the corner and began pushing them into the gutter with a shiny new aluminum snow shovel.

"Now that's really sweet," said the cop. "Priceless." He looked over at me, as if he was waiting for some kind of reaction. When I gave him none, he hustled off to intercept the shoveler.

There was some conversation I couldn't hear, some pointing and shrugging and less-than-polite gesturing, and a baton poked in the kid's chest a few times. Finally the kid took his shovel and went back the way he had come. As he flipped the bird to the cop behind his back, I noticed he wasn't wearing any gloves. I also noticed that he hadn't been shoveling the whole sidewalk, merely the strip where the footprints had been. Or was that my imagination? The cop didn't seem to notice or care. He came stomping back to me, looking like Moses coming down off the mountain, with fire in his eye and heavy indictments on his mind.

"You know," he said, "after fifteen years on the job, I've developed a terrific memory for faces. You look exactly like the guy I just told to get his ass out of here." He must have had a circulation problem in his left hand, because he was rhythmically beating on his gloved palm with his nightstick now.

"I can identify the victim," I said.

"You said you didn't see anything." The baton came out of his left hand, and both it and he were suddenly at full cock.

"I didn't, but I know the dead man."

"Is that all? Well, it so happens that I also know him. That's why they call this my turf, you know? He's a bum named Cee Vee, a nobody, lives in a box down in some boofug Dogpatch ditch. And some cokeheads or meth freaks decided to punch his lights out and then liked it so much that they just couldn't stop themselves. Case closed."

"His name was Charles Victor," I said.

"The hell, you say. Now you can give me yours." He took out his notebook and flipped it to a page that looked like as if it was already full of doodles and phone numbers.

"Herman Jackson."

He started to write, and I peered over the edge of the pad enough to see if he had written Charlie's name, too.

"You're starting to piss me off, Herman Jackson. You want to know the remedy for that?"

"No."

"That's good, because—"

"Did you get the name of the kid with the shovel?"

"Jesus, you just don't take a hint, do you? He's a kid with a shovel, okay? Another nobody, also saw nothing. The guy that owns the hardware store around the corner gave him five bucks to shovel the walk, he says. Big mystery. You happy now? Get the hell out of here."

"Did you notice he wasn't wearing any gloves?"

"Your point?" He stopped writing, sighed, and gave me a pained look.

"Would you be out shoveling with no gloves?"

"No." He stuck the notebook back in his pocket and pointed the baton menacingly at my chest. "What I'd be doing, is I'd be over here trying to get rid of some smartass wants to tell me my job. Some guy who's about to get smacked for his trouble, he pushes it just a little bit farther."

"But he—"

"The detectives will be here in a little bit, also trying to tell me my job, and when they do, I do not want you around helping them. Got it?"

I could see I was arguing with a parking meter, so I stuck my hands in my pockets and started to go. "There is one thing the detectives are going to want you to have found out," I said over my shoulder.

I took three steps back across the street and was stopped by the handle end of the black baton, hooked over my shoulder.

"You got one shot," said the cop. "One. What are they going to want me to know?"

"There is no hardware store around the corner. There's nothing but the back doors of a lot of offices and a hole-in-the-wall shoe repair shop."

"Look, the kid said—"

"Wow, you don't suppose he lied to a cop, do you? Why would he do that?"

"Shit," said the cop. "Sam bitch! Listen, mister smartass Herman Jackson, you do not talk to the detectives, you got that? You do *not*." Then he spun on his heel and ran off in the direction of the now-shoveled street corner, shouting into his radio on the way.

It seemed to me he had a lot of funny attitudes for a cop. It also seemed that he didn't know his own turf very well. Or else he belonged there even less than I did. I tagged along behind, just to see what the detectives were not supposed to.

But when I rounded the corner, the street was empty. I walked a bit farther, to put the street light behind me, and squinted into the darkening urban landscape. Two blocks away, cop, kid, and shovel were running away as fast as they could. They were already far enough off to be hard to see clearly, but it sure looked as if they were together, rather than one chasing the other. Another quick block, a turn into a side street or alley, and they were gone.

I went back the way I had come, turned the corner again, and looked over at the crime scene. The first squad car was just arriving. The first one. And I knew, absolutely, that the cop I had talked to wasn't coming back.

I wanted to kick myself for being so slow on the uptake. It had puzzled me when I said I knew the victim, and instead of getting interested, the cop got pissed. That's not how cops are supposed to act. It should have set off my radar. And I should have also wondered how this guy just happened to get to the scene so fast.

Should have.

I didn't go back toward the body, to tell a new set of cops who the victim was. For all I knew, the uniform I had talked to was really a cop, and if so, I wasn't sure how I should play the scene. Whatever the guy was, I was sure he had at least witnessed the murder, if not had a hand in it. Sticky. You don't hand off that kind of information unless you're sure of the people you're handing it to.

Instead, I headed back to Lefty's to find Wilkie and see if he was carrying. Because if I was going to try to follow Officer Pissed Off and his shovel-toting friend, I definitely wanted a gun in my pocket.

◇◇◇

Wilkie was gone when I got back to the pool hall, so I borrowed a piece from Lefty, despite his being not all that happy about the idea.

"I get held up while you're off with that, I expect you to make good on my losses," he said.

"You get held up a lot, do you?"

"What's that got to do with anything?"

"That's what I thought." I retrieved my leather coat from the rack by the door and stuffed the gun in the pocket. It was a short-barrel .38 revolver, and if Lefty could hit a robber with it from anything more than three feet away, he was a damn sight better shot than I was. But it was what he had. A street preacher I know called The Prophet would say the karma of the moment was structured that way, which was not so different from my Uncle Fred telling me to play the hand I was dealt. Either way, I went with it.

We don't really have a part of town called Nighttown, but that's how I always think of it. East of downtown and north of what's left of the old Soo Line freight yards and the warehouses they used to service, the land falls away sharply to a low, weedy area that never quite knew what to do with itself except be a place for the Mississippi to flood into every spring. A bit north of there, the general slough forks into two distinct branches, Swede Hollow to the east and Connemara Gulch to the west. The high ground between those two is called Railroad Island. The buildings suddenly get a lot seedier and farther apart there than in downtown, mixed with scattered vacant lots and impromptu junkyards that are overgrown with weeds and favored by strange animals and stranger people. There are still a few shacky houses and apartments and some small industrial buildings, like plating factories and chop shops, but a lot of the area is just wilderness. The urban removal programs of the sixties wiped out most of the old slum housing and marginal businesses and replaced them with nothing. I guess somebody thought that was progress.

Neither of the gulches is a good place to go alone and after dark. The high ground may or may not be any better, depending on which alley you go down. A deputy sheriff friend of mine first got me calling it Nighttown because, she says, there are a lot of ways for your lights to go out there, ways that have nothing to do with the sun going down. Somewhere down there, "under the wye-duct," Charlie may have had his cardboard box, the one that wasn't warm enough. And that general direction was where the cop and the kid with the shovel seemed to be headed. And though I knew he was still lying on the sidewalk across from Lefty's, I had the strong feeling that somewhere down there, Charlie was waiting for me. Waiting for me to set things right.

Nighttown

The cop and the kid had a big head start on me by the time I got back from Lefty's, but rush hour had been over for a long time and the snow continued to fall, so there weren't a lot of competing footprints to confuse things. I followed them east for four or five blocks, then north and east, across a bridge over the Interstate ditch and into an area of old factories and warehouses, somewhere near Railroad Island. The streetlights got very far apart there, and about a block past the bridge, they disappeared completely. I was beginning to wish I had hit Lefty up for a flashlight as well as a piece.

Over behind an old industrial building that had been partly made into artists' lofts and partly abandoned to squatters, some street people were huddled around a trash fire in an old barrel. They were a younger and tougher-looking bunch than the usual pack of lost souls and dehorns that hang around in that area, and if I'd been smart, I'd have probably just kept walking. But there was no more pristine snow, and no more distinct tracks. They were my last hope for picking up the trail again.

I headed over to see what I could learn from the great unwashed.

"Here comes another one."

"Another what?" A second shapeless bundle of rags looked up from the fire.

"Sit-ee-zen, man, what you think?"

"Nah, this one ain't no citizen. This one ain't got no ramrod up his ass, like that last dude."

"Bet he ain't got no badge, neither."

"Does he gots money, is what the thing is."

"I can think of some ways to find out."

"Think of one that don't get us all busted."

"Shit, man."

"Shit is right. You think I'm playin' y'all here?"

"Shit."

That seemed to be the consensus, all right.

There were five of them altogether, and I found their talk about *another* sit-ee-zen more than a bit interesting. But before I was likely to hear any more of it, there was some physical protocol to take care of. A little respect, a little threat, a little reward. Not the way the cops do it. Let them know you're not afraid of them, but let them wonder if they should be afraid of you. Easy, easy. First, though, find a place where they can't get behind you.

I caught the eye of the big black guy who was doing most of the talking, held up my last twenty from the pool game, and let him get a good look at it. Then I went over to a niche in the back of the closest industrial building, an inside corner by a loading dock. He looked at his buddies as if wanting their approval. They didn't react, which was good news. It meant they probably weren't a regular gang. The big guy shuffled over to me, and the others followed about five yards back.

"Rough night to be out," I said.

"'Pends on if you with you friends, man."

"Yeah, well it's always good to have friends," I said. I took the .38 out of my pocket and let my arm hang by my side, partially lost in the folds of my coat. Then I rotated the piece outward, toward him, giving him just a bit of a look.

"I'm real scared, man. So what you lookin' for, with your big-assed strap and your little bitty double sawbuck?"

"Two guys, a cop and a big kid, came by here maybe fifteen minutes ago, tops."

"You shittin' me? That's it? You ain't lookin' for ol' Cee Vee's squat?"

That got my attention, but I tried not to show it too much. I tore the twenty in half and gave him one piece of it.

"First, the cop and the kid," I said.

"For that crappy piece of paper? Go fuck yourself."

"Listen, man, what's your name?"

He glared at me for a while, just to show me he didn't have to tell me if he didn't want to. Then he did it anyway.

"Linc."

"Okay Linc, tell me. You know about the stick and the carrot?"

"What's that, some rock group?"

"That's the two things you can get, to make you feel like talking to me. Twenty is all the carrot I've got. After that's gone, we go to the stick. Trust me, you don't want that."

"You a cop?" said one of the other worthies, who was sidling his way up to me along the dock face.

Didn't I wish? If I were a cop, I could call for backup. I took a deep breath and tried again.

"No. I'm also not a fed or a social worker or a preacher or a politician. And that means I don't have anybody I report to or any damn procedure I have to follow. Think about that for a minute."

Number three continued to crowd in on me, and the momentum started going the way I had hoped to avoid. Oh, well.

I made a sudden jerky movement, as if I were trying to get away from the guy. He took that as an invitation, which it was, to stick out an arm and lunge for me. I grabbed the arm and pulled him in the direction he was already moving, only a lot faster than he wanted to go. As he lurched by, I kicked his legs out from under him, letting him sprawl on the ground in front of me. Then I put one foot on his neck, hard, swung Lefty's .38 up into full view, and pointed it at the guy who had been moving in from the other way.

"Five guys, six bullets," I said. "I can make that work. Or you can all split an easy twenty bucks and get the hell out of here." With my left hand, I waved the torn bill in front of me. "Your choice. You don't look stupid to me. How do you want to play it?" And I gave them about two seconds of a totally phony smile.

"Cool," said the big one with the other half of my twenty.

"Cool what?"

"What I says is we all play it cool, man." And he held up his hands, palms toward me, and backed away half a step.

"I think you're smarter than your buddy under my foot here," I said. "So how about cop and the kid?"

"Yeah, okay. They come by here, jus' like you say. Then they take a cab."

"What the hell does that mean?"

"Somebody in a big black set of wheels come by and picked them up, is what."

"What kind of wheels?"

"Big, is all I know. Not a stretch, but a 98 of some kind. One of them high mothers."

"Like a SUV? Escalade, maybe?"

"Yeah, maybe. I dunno."

"Was the kid in cuffs?"

"Nah, they was tight, man. Wasn't no bust or shit goin' down. Them rims come for them, is all."

"And which way did the rims go?"

"That way." He pointed toward the gulch, deeper into Railroad Island.

"You're sure? They didn't head back into town?"

"What I said, man. Back that way. That enough?"

"We're getting there. Now tell me why you asked me about Cee Vee's pitch."

"She-it, man, that's the flavor of the day. First a couple of suits come by askin', back this afternoon, a dude and a broad. Broad was bad, too, but she didn't bust a move or nothin' and they didn't pay us. They just flash around these fancy ID cards an' all, wasn't even real badges."

"Feds?"

"Maybe, some kind."

"And who else?"

"Short, fat dude with a big overcoat and a funny hat, maybe two, three hours ago. He didn't have no fancy ID, but he gave us fifty presidents."

"And what did you tell him?"

"You got fifty, man?"

"I already told you I don't. We're almost home free, man. Let's make it work, here."

"Yeah, well, we didn't really have no cipher to give him, no how, so we made up some shit. Kinda like the shit we tole the suits. Tole them Cee Vee's box was down under the viaduct, whatever the fuck that is, 'cause that's what he allus use to say. An' we tole them the viaduct was down in Sheeny Gulch, which who the hell knows?" He hooked a thumb in the general direction behind his back.

"So, what did they all do?"

"Do? What you think, man? They all go down there, is what they all do."

"What about the guy with the ramrod up his ass?"

"Who?"

"Aw, hell, and we were doing so well there." I stuffed the half of the twenty back in my pocket.

"Oh, you mean *that* dude, the one we was talkin' bout when you come up? Looks like a jarhead with a cheap suit? He got out of the wheels."

"The wheels that picked up the—"

"Yeah, yeah, that one."

"And you weren't going to tell me about him?"

"I thought I'd keep the story short, you know? He didn't talk much, no how. I s'pose he coulda been making sure nobody followed the wheels. Thought he was hot shit, gives us a hard stare for a while like he's lookin' to rumble some. Finally he just splits."

"Let me guess…"

"Down to the gulch. It was like a regular fucking parade, man."

"This is good," I said, and I handed the other half of the bill over to him. "Thanks, Linc."

"You gonna let Mingus, there, up?"

"He fuckin' well better," said the head that was down by my foot, "or when he does, I'm unna—" I stepped down a bit harder, and he grunted a bit and then shut up.

"Back off thirty paces, and he's all yours."

They walked backward, back to their trash barrel, and I slowly lifted my foot. Mingus, if that was really his name, pushed himself up fast to a hands-and-knees position, looking pissed. But before he could jump up to his full height, I stuck the barrel of the .38 up against his nose and let him have a good look at it.

"Don't do anything stupid, Mingus."

He stared cross-eyed at the piece for a moment, then shook his head vehemently. I let him get the rest of the way up, and he hustled off to join the others. When they started their own muttered, low conversation again, I turned and walked away, toward the reportedly popular gulch.

I let out the breath I'd been holding for longer than I could remember.

Fifty yards later, I was in a totally unlit area of weeds, rocks, and trash. A short way ahead, it got even darker, as the snow gave way to the utter black of Connemara Gulch, gaping below and beyond me. Or maybe it was just some railroad ditch. I wasn't that sure of where I was anymore. I couldn't tell how far it was to the bottom, but the way down looked steep and treacherous. There had to be a better route. Right or left? I picked left and walked along the edge of the gully for a while, and sure enough, I came to a crude roadway with a gate across it where it dropped down into the hollow. And standing with one hand on the gate was a guy who must have been the ramrod-ass that the village people had liked so much. Stiff posture, military-style brush cut on his light hair, and a dark topcoat that hung on him like a tent that was one size too big. And even in the dark, I could tell he wore a look that said, "I'm in charge here, and you are lower than whale shit." One of my favorite types. I wondered if I could find an excuse to shoot him.

"This road is closed," he said.

No "mister," no "sir," not even a "please." Wow, he really did want to impress me with what a badass he was. And for all I knew, he really was. He was big, anyway. He had his hands shoved deep in his coat pockets, and I had the impression I did not want him to take them out.

"Because you say it is? Who are you, exactly?"

"You have no business here," he said, in non-reply. "Move along."

"I asked who you are," I said.

"I'm Mister Colt." He opened his coat and let me see that he had two semiautomatics in holsters, in addition to a compact submachine gun that he had just pulled out of a pocket. "And your name is Mud. Some people are about to get hurt here, and unless you haul ass now, you could be one of them. This has nothing to do with you."

That was way too much firepower for me. "Thanks for the warning," I said. I kept my hands at my side, turned around and walked back into the shadows.

In the black gulch below, somebody was switching on powerful flashlight beams. They looked as if they were on the bottom of the ocean. Then there was a bunch of shouting that progressively got louder. Some of it sounded hysterical, all of it angry. Soon there were crashing noises to go with it and then sporadic automatic weapons fire.

And there was the smell.

What the hell was it? A gasoline smell of some kind, but not like what you whiff when you fuel up your car. Kerosene, maybe, or the kind of gas they use in camp lanterns.

As I thought about it, the gulch below lit up with the orange glow of tents and sleeping boxes and piles of rags being torched. Somebody, or rather several somebodies, were moving through the gulch, setting fire to everything in sight and driving a frantic clot of ragged derelicts in front of them.

I stared, dumbfounded, transfixed. I felt the hair on the back of my neck stand up, and my ears roared with my own pulse. Why the hell did they have to use fire? I hate fire. Let me die any way but that.

For a while, I watched the pyrotechnics display and the shadowy crowd of refugees move farther down the gulch, away from me. And seeing nothing to be gained down there but trouble, I turned away. I didn't know where Square Head was by then, but I decided he was right: I had no business down there.

As I walked back the way I had come, fresh out of ideas and purpose, I found the snow shovel.

Business as Unusual

The next morning, I blew the dust off the remote for my TV and listened to the early morning news as I worked on my first caffeine fix of the day and my nourishing, balanced breakfast of White Castle hamburgers and bread-and-butter pickles. The incident at the trash barrel bothered me. I had pulled a gun on a man I did not really want to kill, and that can't happen, ever. Once a gun is out, it takes on a life of its own, and all your careful plans for anonymous existence can suddenly be nothing but yesterday's daydreams.

As troubling as all that was, the fires down in the gulch were worse, if only because I had no idea what to make of them. The media, of course, wouldn't know how to tell me the complete or accurate truth if their ratings actually depended on it. But they might at least tell me something about the superficial events. That would be a start.

But the early news said nothing about a commando raid on homeless people or any mysterious fire in Connemara Gulch. On three different channels, male-female anchor teams flirted ever so mildly, giggled at their own inane jokes, chatted about the latest squabbles between the City Council and the Mayor, and offered advice on how to prepare your lawn for winter. They also promised to give me the morning traffic reports and some high-powered weather information after only sixteen or twenty more commercials. I quickly remembered why my remote control is all covered with dust. How can people listen to that shit every day?

Before I left for my office, I called the non-emergency number for the police and got a female desk sergeant with a phone voice that radiated don't-mess-with-me with thorns on it.

"A man named Charles Victor was killed outside Lefty's Pool Hall last night," I said. "I'm wondering if I could talk to the detective who has that case."

"And your name is?"

I told her.

"Are you calling from your own phone?"

"Yes, I am."

"And you have information on what case, again?"

"The murder of Charles Victor." I almost said I didn't have any information, but I could see how far that would get me. As it happened, it didn't make any difference.

"We have no such case on record, sir." If her voice had been any colder, my phone would have been icing up.

"Maybe you just don't have the name. He was a homeless person."

"We have more than one John Doe homicide currently open, sir. Could you give me some more information?"

"This man was beaten to death last night, in front of Lefty's Pool Hall."

"And you were a witness?"

"No. I just have some information about the victim. I'm a bail bondsman, and he used to be a client of mine." I also had the shovel, of course, but somehow I didn't feel like sharing that information with her.

"That would be Detective Erickson's case, sir. He's very busy right now."

"How about if we let him decide that? Could you transfer me, please?"

"I'll tell him you called, sir. If he needs your information, he will get back to you. I have other calls to take here."

"Can I talk to some other detective, then?"

"To which detective did you wish to speak?"

"I have no idea. Any detective."

The line went dead, and I could swear the receiver was flipping me the bird. I wondered what time the shift changed at the cop shop, so I could try again with a different professional asshole. Meanwhile, I wrote down the name of the detective, put on my coat and headed for my car.

Outside, I was able to figure out, even without Super Duper Doppler Radar, that last night's snow was melting, though the sky was the color of dirty dishwater and could spit some more of the stuff at any time. The sun was nowhere in sight and there was just enough wind to get your attention. It was all very October.

I took my usual route downtown and parked the BMW 328i in the Victory Ramp. I mostly park there because I love the name. I like to think Winston Smith would have parked there, if the Thought Police had let him have a car. Then he could have made it with his darling Julia in the back seat, and he wouldn't have had to worry about all those nasty rats. It may not be great literature that way, but it's a favorite fantasy.

Walking from the ramp to my office, I bought copies of both the *St. Paul Pioneer Press* and the *Minneapolis Star and Tribune* from some paperboys disguised as tin boxes. If they contained anything about the fires in the gulch, it wasn't on the front page of either. A quick flip of pages showed me that it also wasn't on the first page of the Local News sections. What on earth was going on here? The *Strib* was often a day late in reporting local events on this side of the river, though they sometimes made up for it with better detail. But the *Pioneer* should have caught it. Hell, it was practically in their back parking lot. On a slow news day, which it was, it should have made big headlines. Or Charlie's murder should have.

As usual, Agnes, my indispensable Lady Friday, general manager, and confidante was at the office ahead of me. I think she does that just to make me feel guilty. She isn't aware of this, of course. Someday I'll explain it to her.

She had already opened the mail and was having a nice dia-
logue with her computer, while off in another corner, Mr. Coffee
was talking to himself in some belchy-gurgly appliance creole.

I threw the newspapers on my desk, hung up my coat, and
picked up a letter from the top of the stack. It was hand written
on three sheets of lined yellow legal paper, the kind that cops give
perps to write their confessions. The assault upon the language
spoke for itself, but at least it wasn't in crayon. And it was fairly
polite, in its own way. It also came in a neat white envelope and
was actually legible.

Agnes smirked when I picked it up. Not a good sign. I
smoothed out the smudged paper and read:

Dear Mr. Jackson Bail Bonds
    I am writing about a bond you sold me that din't work.
I mean, they let me out of jail and all, even though I had
to come back later, but I din't enjoy it. I found out my
woman run off with the bus driver lives down stairs from
us if you can believe that shit and I din't have no money
to go get some ass or some booze on account of the bond
and the lawyer. So my brother he come home from the
U S Army where he was on absence of leave and I told
him how I wasn't getting none and even if I was to get
unconvicted, I'd have to give the lawyer a bunch more
money, too, which I ain't got. So him and me we got all
sad together and then we got some Colt 45 and got all
lickered up a little and decided to go rob the Army Navy
Surpluss Store on Payne Avenue. Just to even things up,
like. But there was a alarm in the store, wun't you know,
and we got caught and now I'm back in the slam, and my
brother too. And because of the first bond I can't get no
new one cause there dam sure pissed at me this time.
    So I just thought. I no you ecsplained to me that I don't
never get my bond money back, not in anny real money
or nothing. But I thought maybe since the first bond din't
work and I ain't got no more money since we got caught

before we finished robbing the Army Navy Surpluss store, maybe you could see your way clear to make a free bail bond for my brother so he can get out of this awful place and go back to the U S Army and go get his self killed in some forn country like Irack, like a real solder. He is a good man and it seems like the least you could do for your country any how.

I hope I don't have to add that I still have lots of friends on the out side who can find out where you live, if you no what I mean.

My brother's name is Vitrol, like the hair tonic, and last name same as mine. Help him out, can you, and we will be all square again.

Your frend in boundage,
Remo Wilson but my friends call me Trick

God, I love this business. It's not the money; it's the class of people you get to meet. I snatched a cup of coffee from the gurgling machine, pouring it quickly so not too much would drip onto the hot bottom plate. The plate hissed at me from under the pot, telling me I hadn't been quick enough.

I looked over the letter again. I could only count it as another triumph for the adult literacy program at the County Workhouse.

"Why do you always have to do that?"

"That? What that?"

"Pour yourself a cup of coffee before it's done brewing."

"Oh that that. Because it's better then. And a lovely good morning to you, too, Agnes. Know anything about lifting fingerprints?"

"Of course it's better then. That's because all the gunky, bitter stuff is in the last cup that drips through. Good morning."

"Then maybe we should shut it off before it gets to that part." I took a sip and found the morning's brew, as expected, really rather good. Later, it would be progressively more like battery acid.

"Sometimes it's abundantly clear to me why you're not married, Herman. Fingerprints off what, the coffee pot?"

"No, off a snow shovel." *It had better not be abundantly clear, or I'm in a lot of trouble.*

"You can't be serious."

She went back to pecking at her keyboard, which is a sure sign that she sees she's talking to a crazy person and would really rather not deal with it just now, thank you. Or maybe she was disappointed that I wasn't going to talk about the deeply moving letter from my friend in boundage, Trick.

I noticed, not for the first time, that she actually looked her best with a mild mock scowl, concentrating on her computer through a pair of thick glasses. Agnes is a hard person to describe, even harder to remember, somehow. It's as if she had no prominent features to focus on. I had known her for eight years, and I still looked at her and tried to remember who it was she reminded me of. She had one of those oddly familiar faces that are neither young nor old, always pleasant but a bit self-deprecating, almost perky, almost pretty, almost sexy. Almost. Sometimes I wonder if I ought to be closer to her, but I'm not. And sometimes I wonder if she would like to change all that. But then I forget to wonder more. She definitely looked nice, though, scowling through her glasses.

"Of course I'm serious," I said. "In the movies, they're always talking about dusting something for prints, right?"

"Yes they are. So?"

"So, what's the dust?"

"How should I know? Fluorescent bath talc, probably."

"That sounds reasonable. Got any?"

If looks could kill, my day would have ended, right then and there. I decided to change the subject.

"I got my Visa statement yesterday."

"Does that have something to do with fingerprints?"

"No, that has to do with you not cashing your last two paychecks."

"Well, what did you expect? You can't be writing payroll on credit, Herman. That's worse than going to a loan shark."

"No, it's not. Visa won't break my legs if I don't pay them."

"Herman, it's economic suicide."

"More like slightly postponed disaster. Trust me, Ag, I can afford to go into debt better than you can afford to go without being paid." I really couldn't, but my only other options at the moment were to sell the BMW or go into one of my secret escape caches.

"Look, Herman, we can…"

Her voice trailed off as she was distracted by something out in the street, and her expression changed from plain vanilla anxiety to real, double Dutch resentment.

"Here comes trouble," she said.

I turned to follow her gaze and saw a shapeless middle-aged guy in a sharp brown pinstripe. He crossed the street against the light without looking to either side, as if he either didn't care about getting run down or simply expected everybody to get out of his way. Once across, he looked up, turned, and headed toward my door. I had never seen him before.

"Friend of yours, Aggie?"

"Not on the best day he ever had. He's been here a few times, looking for you."

He was not a big man, but he had a certain presence, and his round face seemed on the verge of a sneer, as if he knew he intimidated people and was glad of it. He wore what was left of his brown hair slicked straight back under a classic dark fedora, a hat so out, it was back in again, and he walked with his lump of a chin out, as if it were a badge of authority. He dressed expensively but with just a touch too much flash, I thought, like somebody who spends all his time running away from an impoverished past. Or maybe some street muscle who has just graduated to middle management and doesn't yet know how to shop. He didn't look as if he was carrying, but his suit coat was cut large at the chest, possibly to hide the occasional holster.

He let himself in, and when he spoke, his voice was gravel and oil, with a certain smugness to it and an accent I couldn't quite identify. Some sub-species of New Yorker, possibly.

"Mr. Jackson?"

"The very one." Following Agnes' lead, I did not offer him my hand, but I did give him the courtesy of not glaring.

"My name is Eddie Bardot, Mr. Jackson, I represent—"

"The mob," said Agnes.

"Oh, please." He gave me a stage smile and held up his hands in a palms-forward gesture of innocence. "Let's not get melodramatic here, shall we?" He jerked a thumb at Agnes and said, "Missy Four Eyes here doesn't like me coming around your office. I think she's afraid I might make a pass at her."

And I swear to God, he gave me a wink. I didn't think anybody ever did that anymore. I was not charmed by it, nor by the fact that he liked to stand less than two feet away when he talked to me.

"You can take your 'missy' and your 'four eyes' and go wander off a cliff somewhere," said Agnes. For her, that was pretty nasty, and I wondered what this guy had said to her in my absence.

"Maybe we should talk privately," he said to me.

"Maybe we shouldn't. How about if you just quit talking about Agnes as if she weren't here, and we'll see how that works? And back off, while you're at it. We're not conspirators or lovers, so get out of my space."

He backed off a step, but not as far as I would have liked.

"All right, look, maybe we all got off on the wrong foot here. Let's try again, okay? I represent…"

He looked pointedly at Agnes, to see if she was going to interrupt him again, but she merely stared at him with one eyebrow raised.

"I represent," he went on, "a, um *group* of businessmen who are investing heavily in the bail bond business. You have a very nice little operation here, Mr. Jackson, but the word is, you have a cash flow problem."

"Oh really? And whose word would that be?"

"With a bigger block of capital, see, and some better connections, some better layoff options, you could be—"

"Squeezed out," said Agnes.

"I thought she wasn't going to interrupt me."

"I didn't hear her say that. I thought you weren't going to talk about her as if she weren't here."

"Could I please just finish what I came here to tell you?" The color was starting to rise in his face now, the veneer of civility beginning to wear thin. *Silk over slime*, I thought. *Soon it will begin to seep through.* But he went on in almost the same tone, with just a bit more open hostility now.

"You're a successful businessman, Jackson. You know what that means in this day and age?"

"You bet. It means I can be fussy about who I talk to."

"It means," and he paused slightly and drew himself up to his full height, "that you are a prime candidate for being bought out. In case you don't know it, that's a very big deal."

"Oh, I can see that, all right."

"You think I'm joking? That's the American dream now. Nobody tries to make it on their own anymore. The real jackpot is when you get successful enough that the big boys want your operation. And they do."

"And why do I care what they want?"

"Oh, you care, believe me. You're about to find out how much you care. Anyway, you never think about retiring young? No more sweating the recovery rate of your bounty hunters? No more wondering if anybody knows you only run an eighty percent layoff rate? Think of all the trips you'd like to take, maybe with—"

"Don't even think about using that phrase again," said Agnes.

"What she said," I said. "Just who are these so-called big boys, by the way?"

Bardot reached into an inside pocket and produced a business card, which he handed to me with what I'm sure he thought was a significant look. It was an expensive-looking, low-key bit of embossed printing, and under his name, it said "Amalgamated Bonding Enterprises." Without an "Inc.," I noted.

"This tells me diddly squat," I said. "I'd like to know just exactly who all these wonderful, amalgamated, unincorporated folks are." I stuck the card in my shirt pocket without being properly awed by it.

"Oh, big people. Very big, very important. Venture capitalists, entrepreneurs. Totally above reproach."

"Who?"

"Well, they like to keep a low profile. You know how it is."

"No. How is it?"

"Mind your own damn business, is how it is." Finally, the smile was completely gone, the gloves off. "This is a real opportunity here, Jackson."

"You're absolutely right."

"Excuse me?"

"About minding my own business. That's what it is. My business. And that's what it stays. It's not for sale and it's not open to extortion."

"Everything is for sale, Jackson. And everybody has their pressure points."

"In your world, maybe. So what happens now? Do you send Guido and Dutch over here to tip over my vegetable stand and break my windows, just to show me you're serious?"

"Do you really take me for a thug, Jackson?"

"'I would you were so honest a man.'"

"What's that supposed to mean?"

"It means get the hell out of here."

He sighed and turned around. "It always starts this way," he said. And without waiting for my brilliant retort, he left, once again crossing the street against the light and without looking either way.

"Nice fellow," I said, "but very confused."

"How did he know about your layoff rate, do you suppose?"

"You picked up on that, too, did you, Aggie?"

"He made it hard to miss."

"It could be a guess on his part," I said, not really believing it, "but if so, it hit awfully close to the truth. I'm sure that's one of the things he wants us to contemplate while he's gone."

"I take it you're expecting him back."

"Oh, I think we can count on that. And the next time, he'll have something to up the ante with."

"What do you think his 'big, important people' really want, Herman? Is this whole act really just simple extortion?"

"It's some kind of extortion for sure, but I don't think it's so simple. I'm guessing they really do want to buy my business, but not before they've screwed it up somehow, so it's not worth much of anything."

"I don't like this, Herman."

"You're right, Aggie, you don't like this at all."

The phone rang, and since Agnes was still looking a little stressed out, I picked it up.

"Jackson Bail Bonds."

"Herman?"

"Speaking."

"Yeah, say, Frankie Russo here, Herman. I just wanted to let you know it was nothing personal."

"Of course it wasn't. What are you talking about?"

"Jumping bail."

"Your trial isn't for four days yet."

"Yeah, well I can't be there, is the thing."

"Are you crazy? Failure to appear is a worse offense than the one you're charged with, which is completely bogus anyway. If you hadn't mouthed off to the judge, you'd be ROR. You said it yourself: the cops just want to harass you because they can't legally close down your strip joint like the Mayor so dearly wants them to. If you skip, you'll be doing just what they want."

"Yeah, well, I gotta skip."

"Why on earth?"

"'Cause this guy named Eddie stuck a gun in my face and told me to, is why. He threatened my family, too."

"Son of a bitch."

"Yeah, that would be him, all right. Look, I gotta go, okay? You take care."

"Hey, wait—" The line went dead.

Frank Russo's bond was for twenty-five thousand. And because he was no flight risk at all, I had carried it on my own.

"Call Wilkie and tell him we've got a jumper for him."

Layoffs and Other Labor Problems

It's a funny business, writing bail bonds. People like to say it's like the insurance business, but it's not. Except when it is. In any absolute sense, I'm usually not a bondsman, but a bonding agent, in exactly the same way that the guy you buy your car insurance from is an insurance agent. He doesn't personally insure your car; he just represents a big company that does. And that is what the pinstripe goon, Bardot, was talking about when he referred to laying off the bonds.

The thing is, he wouldn't have used that term for it unless he had some kind of background in a different business altogether. Like bookmaking. "Laying off" a bet is what a bookie calls it when he has somebody make a legitimate bet at a legitimate track, to insure himself against a nasty loss on some suddenly popular long shot or other. And the fact that Bardot used that term meant that he also knew I would be familiar with it. And he wanted me to know that he knew.

He also knew how much of it I did. Laying off, that is. Nobody lays off everything, because there are some clients that are just no risk at all, and you may as well carry them on your own and pocket the full bond fee. Like Frank Russo. There are others that just don't fit any legitimate, regular profile, though they are still perfectly good customers. Those you also carry on your own, if only because you can't sell them to your backup company.

And then there are the bail junkies.

You can't daisy-chain insurance policies. That is, you can't buy a policy against having your roof blow off, say, and when the roof *does* blow off, buy another one against getting water damage, and when that happens too, because now you have no roof, get still another one against getting sick off the mildew and mold, and so on. What sane person would write such a string of policies?

A bail bondsman, that's who. He can make a lot of money at that game, because strange as it sounds, there are people who are bail junkies, and they really, really want that daisy chain. It's almost as if they don't know they're free unless they have to keep paying for it.

So Bud Everett, for example, a good customer of mine, gets busted for getting falling-down drunk and painting some rather uncomplimentary things on the Mayor's car, after he accidentally breaks the rear window and mistakes the back seat for a urinal. That's not what the citation says, of course, but that's the important part. And because it's the Mayor's car and not yours or mine, everybody knows good old Bud is going to do some time.

To that end, the arraigning judge sets bail at five thousand dollars, which he knows damn well Bud can't raise. In any sort of just world, that would be a direct violation of the Eighth Amendment to the US Constitution, but we passed some quibbling laws a long time ago to make the issue of unreasonable bail go away. Nowadays bail is supposed to be unreasonable. That's what it's for.

But even though Bud couldn't raise five thou to buy his soul back from the Devil, he somehow manages to come up with five hundred, which he uses to buy a five-K bond from me. Which obliges me to insure his appearance in court, right?

Wrong.

Also wrong is the idea that I'm going to get some kind of security deposit from him so as not to be out anything when the guy craps out on both me and the court. It's a nice thought, but not only would he not know five thousand if it rang his doorbell looking like Ed McMann, he also very much does not own a thing in the world that's worth that much. His beat-up car probably has more than that against it in outstanding parking fines.

But I write the bond anyway, because Bud Everett is one of my regular nonviolent, nontoxic, recidivist bail junkies.

When his trial date comes up, he fails to appear, as I had no doubt he would. Or rather, wouldn't. That should mean that I or my layoff bonding company, if I had used one, has to cough up the full five thousand dollars.

But the thing is, the court doesn't really want the money, they want *him*. So they give me ten days to produce the little nimrod, figuring I know where to find him, which I do because he's an old regular. He's out in his ex-brother-in-law's old junker of a camping trailer, in the woods up by Forest Lake. He's drinking boilermakers and watching soap operas and bitching to anybody who will listen, which mostly means his dog, Thumper, about how he doesn't want to go to court because he knows he will get a raw deal and he didn't really mess up the Mayor's car all *that* bad, and the asshole had it coming anyway.

So I send Wide Track Wilkie out to talk to him. He works as a bounty hunter when he's not shooting pool, and he persuades Bud that he really ought to do the standup thing, if he wants to retain the ability to stand up, period. And they both go off to the courthouse together.

But not to trial.

He's already missed his slot in the court schedule. That's how this whole scenario got started in the first place. And since there are always more candidates than slots, it has been given to some other worthy. His original trial will now have to be rescheduled and he will be informed of the new date by postcard, no less. That's if he's still walking around free. But what he's in court for *this time* is to get arraigned for jumping bail, or FTA, failure to appear.

That's not as bad an offense as the first one, since it didn't involve the mayor's car and also since he didn't try to run away when Wilkie went to pick him up. So this time bail is set at a mere one thousand, for which Bud can buy a bond from me for another hundred. I have no idea where he gets the extra c-note and probably don't want to know, but he does, and the game begins.

That's right, it merely begins.

The next time his court date comes up, Bud will again be in a drunken pout, since that's the only way he has of dealing with authority, and he will again fail to appear. And once again, Wilkie will go have a little heart-to-heart chat with the lad and bring him downtown for yet another arraignment. And with the backlog in the courts showing no sign of ever getting caught up, this scene can now replay itself roughly every one or two months, for just about forever. That means that for as long as good old Bud does not decide to face up to all his past charges or, even less likely, get a sudden flash of ambition and flee the jurisdiction, he will pay me an average of about fifty dollars a month to be permanently bonded.

And the absolutely hilarious thing is that he will find this a perfectly acceptable arrangement.

I have anywhere from one to a dozen clients like Bud at any given time, and while you can't get rich off them, they can definitely help pay the rent between the big customers. And at the moment, I dearly wished I had a bunch more.

But somebody named Amalgamated Greedy Guys, or whatever the hell it was, wanted them all, enough to scare off one of my clients. Or maybe they just wanted a big slug of money to make them go away and lose interest in me.

"When hell freezes over."

"Excuse me?" said Agnes.

"Talking to myself again," I said. "Sorry. Probably means I forgot to take my meds."

"There are worse problems to have, Herman." She gave me a sort of indulgent big-sister kind of smile.

"Yes there are. And we probably have them, too. Here come some more suits. More gangsters, you suppose?"

She looked out the window, to where I was gesturing with my coffee cup.

"They look more like government," she said. "Feds, I'd guess."

"I believe that's what I said." I opened the door for our new guests, a tallish, athletic-looking man and woman, maybe late thirties, in matching black business suits. The guy wore a dark red tie, the woman a black velvet choker with a tiny cameo pin. Other than that, they looked pretty much the same, except that her legs were better, and I was glad she let them show. Both of them—the people, not the legs—wore tight-lipped expressions that showed they took themselves very seriously.

"Mr. Jackson?" Her voice was deep and throaty, as if she routinely took just a bit too much Dewar's in the evenings, and she had a heart-shaped face with puffy lips that seemed made for whispering. But her manner was all business. Oh, well. Another perfectly good fantasy, shot right to hell. I wondered if this could be the pair of feds my trash-barrel informant had been talking about.

"I'm Herman Jackson. How can I help you?" I held out my hand, but instead of shaking it, the Persons in Black held up some kind of plastic ID cards. Feds, definitely.

Not FBI, though, but Secret Service. I was surprised. Did the President need a bail bond?

"I'm Agent Krause," she said, "and this is my partner, Agent Sladky. We are informed that you, Mr. Jackson, are the bonding agent for one Charles Victor."

"Was," I said.

"Excuse me?"

"I was his bonding agent. He was murdered last night."

Agnes dropped her hands in her lap and gave me a look of wide-eyed astonishment. The two agents were unreadable.

"Then you owe him no further service." She said it without pause or hesitation, as if she had rehearsed the speech. I had no idea what she was driving at.

"I didn't owe him any prior service, either," I said. "He hasn't been bonded by me since the last time he got sent to the Ramsey County Workhouse, last winter. How is it you know about me being his agent, by the way?"

She ignored the question completely. "Whether he had a bond or not, you were holding something for him, I believe?"

"You mean some kind of standing security object?" I shook my head. "When he needed a bond, Charlie always gave me cash for security. And when he got out of the Workhouse, he took it back."

"If he had that kind of money, why would he come to you for a bond at all? Why would he come to anybody for one? That's not even a good lie." Agent Sladky should have continued to let his partner do the talking. He had a slightly nasal, high-pitched voice that made him seem too young for the job. His comment about the lie didn't help any in that department, either. Was there any experienced G-man or cop who didn't expect to be routinely lied to by everybody?

"He didn't trust the court to give him his money back again. He didn't trust any government of any kind, period." I shrugged, to show them that it was Charlie's choice entirely and also a matter of great indifference to me if they believed it or not.

And in any case, I really didn't have any of his money at the moment.

The woman took over again, and I had to admit that I liked hearing her speak. "Well, then, Mr. Jackson, if you will just turn over your files on the man to us, we won't bother you any further. The originals. All of them. You may keep your own copies, of course, but we require the originals. Oh, and any other little item you may have been holding for him, your denial notwithstanding."

"No."

"I beg your pardon?"

"I said 'no.' That means no."

"People do not find it wise to say no to the Secret Service, Mr. Jackson." She eyed me in exactly the way a hawk looks at a very small mouse.

"Well, I'm seldom accused of being wise."

"We have subpoena and warrant power, you know. For any records we might decide we want to see for any reason, not just his. Think about that for a moment. We can turn your past inside out, if we want to."

"Then I suggest you do so, Agent Krause. Do your warrants usually include permission to burn homeless people out of their camps, by the way?"

"I don't believe I know what you're talking about." But her eyes said otherwise. Both agents' façades of cool, self-assured control had wilted. I thought the guy, Sladky, even looked a bit afraid. The woman mainly looked pissed, but quite possibly that was her regular, default posture.

"How could he possibly know—?"

"He doesn't. Shut up, Agent."

"I told you we shouldn't have gone down there. We could have just as well—"

"Sladky, will you please shut up? We're in front of a subject, you know." To me, she said, "We're done here."

She turned on her heel and headed for the door, and her partner followed. Her shoes had some of those compromise high heels that looked as if they had started out as spikes but had melted and squished. They still clicked importantly when she got to the tiled threshold, though. This was a woman who definitely knew all about creating presence. Mostly a threatening one. I found it interesting, though, that she seemed even more hostile toward her partner than she was toward me.

"You'll be seeing us again," she said without turning around.

"Imagine my anticipation."

They both left without another word, leaving the door open, which I took as a classy substitute for slamming it. I shut it in my most restrained manner, and Agnes and I watched them go.

"Well, you certainly handled that well," she said.

"Thank you." I always like it when she lies for me.

"Can you really stand to have them turn your past inside out, by the way?"

"Not really, but one person trying to strong-arm me was enough in one day, Ag. My willing victim quota was all used up. Mostly, though, I can or can't stand it, depending on how far back they go."

"Uh huh. These are federal agents, Herman. They will go back to when God first created dirt and J. Edgar Hoover used it to blackmail somebody."

"That would definitely be too bad. I was sort of hoping they would get tired of the game before then." After about fifteen years of history, to be exact. I had a squeaky clean record back to 1987, when I first came to St. Paul. One could even say it's so virtuous, it's boring. I worked long and hard to make it that way. But try to look farther back, and you will run into a lot of gaps.

Officially, nominally, Herman Jackson, St. Paul bail bondsman, never convicted, arrested, or even suspected of a major crime, was born in 1953 in Manley, Iowa, a tiny farm town that has now almost entirely vanished into the fields of corn and soybeans around it. Its empty Main Street has only a few boarded up buildings left, and even fewer residents, none of whom remembers me. There were church and school records once, but nobody knows what happened to them. Even the tombstone from which I got my birth date is gone, its little plot of ground now busy pushing up barley or oat stalks. It's a wonderful place to be from, since nobody can ever say for sure that you're not.

A really persistent researcher might conclude that between Manley and St. Paul are just too many blank pages to be believed. Awkward, but hardly damning. And even with the research capacity of the federal government, it would be awfully hard for somebody to find a link back to Detroit and a bonding agency abandoned when its principal was implicated in a murder (innocent, I swear) and an insurance fraud (that's another matter altogether.)

Hard, but not impossible. And somebody who knew exactly what to look for might even find a cold case file in Detroit that points to an even colder case file in Toronto that actually contains my fingerprints, the only place on earth that does, other than St. Paul.

The links are all very convoluted, their discovery highly unlikely. And that's good, because bringing them to light could very well spell the end of life as I know it. Against that eventuality, I keep an escape kit in a locker at the Amtrak depot, plus extra cash in two locations out state. If I ever have to use them, I can never, ever come back.

And if I am too slow in making that decision, I will lose the chance forever. I'm not ashamed to say that scares the hell out of me.

Agnes is the only person who knows anything about any of this, apart from my Uncle Fred, the career bookie who is currently doing hard time in the Michigan's Upper Peninsula and can be trusted to be at least as discreet as any other con. Even Agnes doesn't know all the particulars, though she does know that she may someday have to do a rearguard stalling action while I make myself nonexistent. She gets all teary when we talk about it, so I seldom do.

"What about that other thing, Herman? Are we holding anything for Charlie Victor?"

"Nothing that they would really care about."

"Then what's the big deal? Let's give them his files and wave goodbye as they leave."

"It's a matter of principle, Ag. Never give bullies what they want."

"Even when they have the authority to demand it?"

"Especially then."

Massé and Fugue

Athletes like to talk about muscle memory. You make the perfect free throw or the ace tennis serve or the flawless triple axel, the theory goes, and you should immediately do twenty or a hundred more. Then when crunch time comes, even if your mind has degenerated into a useless collage of past disasters, your body remembers how to make the moves.

That's what they say.

I had no idea what I was going to do about my cash flow problems or the pinstriped mobster or the feds whom I had deliberately pissed off or the flames I had seen from Railroad Island or even about Charlie Victor's cigar box, which I had told nobody about, not even Agnes. So I decided to work on the problem that I at least knew how to approach. If the athletes are right, that is.

I left the office and headed back to Lefty's, to practice the pool shot that sooner or later I would have to perform for Wilkie, or else give him his twenty bucks as a forfeit. I can do things like take unscheduled time off, because I own the business. Hard working, sweet-hearted Agnes can't, because she doesn't. Life is not fair.

I gave Lefty back his .38 and got an arched eyebrow and a pointed look at his watch in return. Then I got a large mug of beer, a bowl of salted-in-the-shell peanuts, and a rack of balls, and I rented a table that was as far from Lefty's perch at the bar as I could get. I told him I wanted to be left alone to practice. What I really meant was that I didn't want him noticing me practicing a shot that is famous for turning a cue ball into a deadly airborne missile and also for ripping up the felt on the table. In fact, a lot of pool halls have signs on the wall prohibiting massé shots.

"What are you practicing?"

"Three-cushion banks."

"Wow. Tough stuff."

He didn't know the half of it.

I left the rack with eleven balls in it on a windowsill, putting only the cue ball, the eight, and three striped balls on the table. I picked the shortest cue stick I could find and chalked the tip until there was a little cloud of blue dust floating around it. Then I swallowed a slug of beer, put an unshelled peanut in my mouth so I could suck on the salt, and began.

I started out with a simple draw shot, hitting the cue ball below center and giving it enough backspin to go straight away from me, then change its mind and come straight back. It didn't work very well. The amount of backspin I was able to give the ball was different every time. I pulled an emery board out of my pocket, turned my back to Lefty to hide what I was doing, and proceeded to rough up the cue tip. After that and some more chalk, it worked a lot better. I got in the habit of chalking after every shot, which everybody knows you should always do anyway and nobody ever does.

I did a dozen more draw shots, progressively increasing the angle of the cue stick with the horizontal. As it approached dead vertical, I could get the ball to come back beyond the place where it had started. Sometimes it skipped and bounced a little along the way and sometimes it wobbled a bit, but mostly it worked.

This was pretty exciting stuff. I wondered if they knew about it at MIT or Cal Tech.

It was also pretty trivial, compared to what I had come here to try. I took another slug of beer, shelled and ate a bunch of nuts just to stall a little longer, and finally got down to hitting the ball off-center in two directions at once.

That's kind of a slippery concept, and it doesn't do to think about it too much. But not thinking about it wasn't working worth sour owl shit, either. I could get the ball to go away to the right and come back to the left or vice-versa, but there was no way I could get it to go away *a little* to the left and come back even more to the left.

I decided it was all a matter of point of view, and I tried the shot with the cue in the same place but with me facing a different way. That was a little better.

Finally, I set up all five balls in their original locations, closed my eyes for a moment, and meditated on the mystical state of being Minnesota Fats and a Zen archery master, all at once. Then I tried the massé shot exactly fifty times. I almost made it twice. The odds were getting better, though I seriously doubted if my muscles had learned a thing yet. I decided it was time for another beer.

As I was heading back to the bar with my empty mug, I was met by a short, pasty-faced blimp in a rumpled three-piece sharkskin suit and a striped dress shirt with a pin collar. He also had a hat that I don't know how to describe. A real independent thinker. I hadn't seen pin collars since the mid-nineties, or sharkskin since never mind when. And I had never seen a hat like that, though I thought it might have been what was once described as a pork pie.

"I was told I might find Herman Jackson here. Would that be you?"

"That would be me, yes." *And I was told a fat guy in a suit and a hat went down in the gulch last night. Would that be you?* "And you are?"

"G. Harold Mildorf, Attorney at Law. My card." He pulled a business card out of his vest pocket, showed it to me, and then put it back, just as the Persons in Black had done with their plastic ID cards.

"You have a client who needs a bond, Mr. Mildorf?"

"You mean a bail bond? Certainly not. I don't practice criminal law. In fact, I try not to even practice civil law with people who might possibly be criminals. Is there someplace private where we could talk?" He looked at the cane-backed spectator chairs around the perimeter of the hall as if they might be about to attack him, his bushy eyebrows nearly meeting as he formed them into a frown.

"Lefty's in the morning is about as private as anything you're liable to find. Pick up a stick and pretend you're shooting pool, and I guarantee you nobody will pay the slightest attention to us." Not that there was anybody else around anyway.

He obviously didn't like the idea, but he took a cue stick off a rack on the wall and walked back to the table. I suddenly became aware of the empty beer mug in my hand.

"I was just going to get myself another beer. Would you like anything?"

"Do they have food?"

"They have the usual bar food. Fried stuff, microwave pizza, that sort of thing. The burgers are pretty good."

"I'll have two burgers and fries and a large beer."

"The beer, I'll get you. The other stuff, I'll order, and Lefty will bring it over when it's ready."

"Lefty. So there really is such a person. How fearsomely droll."

"You're holding the cue stick by the wrong end, by the way." I left him to ponder the subtle geometry of tapered wood and went back to the bar, where I ordered his little snack.

"On your tab?" said Lefty.

"No way. I don't even know this guy."

"Oh yeah? Well, he knows you. He was watching you shoot pool last night."

"Really?"

"Almost the whole time. Came in after you'd already started, asked me to point you out. Another beer?"

"I suddenly lost my taste for the light buzz. Give me a new mug of beer for my spectator friend and a cup of coffee for me."

"Is that on your tab or not?"

"The drinks, yes. For everything else, G. Harry there is on his own."

"Got it. I'll collect cash when I bring the stuff."

"Can't say I blame you."

We were talking about a lawyer, after all.

I went back over in the corner and found G. Harold Mildorf pushing the eight ball around the table with his stick, scowling at it in intense concentration.

"I don't believe you've stumbled onto your secret vocation, Mr. Mildorf. There's nobody here to impress, so why don't we just sit down and wait for your food?"

"Really? I thought I was doing rather well."

"Trust me, you don't want to enter any high stakes tournaments." I gestured to a couple of chairs over by the windows, and we ambled over that way and sat down. I found a small round table that was only slightly wobbly and pulled it over in front of us.

"I don't really have any papers to lay out," he said.

"How very un-lawyerlike. But you do have about four and a half pounds of food on the way."

"Oh, yes. Well then, a table by all means."

"While we're waiting for it, why don't you tell me what's on your mind?"

He looked around the entire place, working his mouth in odd ways and squinting, as if some silent spy might have snuck in while we were looking at chairs. Then he leaned over close to me and said in a low, conspiratorial tone, "Charles Victor."

"He's dead." I think I upset him by speaking in a normal voice. He deepened his already monumental scowl.

"The body on the sidewalk?"

I nodded.

"I feared as much. The whole point of my being here, in fact. You see, I am the executor of his estate."

Good thing I wasn't sipping my coffee at the moment, because I would have definitely choked on it.

"Estate? Charlie had an estate?"

"But of course."

"Get the hell out of here."

"Excuse me? My food hasn't arrived yet."

"It's an expression, Mr. Mildorf. It means 'I can't believe what you're saying.'"

"Oh, I see. Get out of the hell, yes, um… Let me assure you, I am entirely in earnest. He had an estate, and you, Mr. Jackson, are his sole heir. I am empowered to give you this." From an inside jacket pocket, he produced two or three pieces of paper that had been folded into business-envelope size. As he handed them over, he again scanned the room in all directions.

"A copy of his will," he said. "Only two pages, and not terribly eloquent. But it definitely names you as his one and only beneficiary. He even mentions his father, someplace up in the northern part of the state, so there can be no question of him merely forgetting that he had one. He mentions him, curses him, and excludes him. All very legal. You get everything, as you can see."

I stuffed the papers in the inside pocket of my suit coat without looking at them.

"Besides his cardboard box and some occasional walking-around money, what does 'everything' consist of, exactly?"

"Ah yes, well, therein lies the problem. I don't honestly know, you see. Not exactly how much, and not where it is, either. I know he had something, because he paid my fee in cash and didn't quibble about the amount. And he claimed to have something he called a frag box, which he said contained thirty thousand dollars, but I never saw it. Aren't you going to read the will?"

"What's the point? Aren't we exactly where we would have been if you had never talked to me?"

"We most certainly are not. I have now delivered the will, as I am legally charged to do. That is not a trivial thing, you know. Don't you at least want look at it?" He pointed with an index finger, looking as if he really wanted to pull the papers back out of my pocket.

"Later, maybe. Tell me about this frag box thing."

"You realize, of course, that if you weren't his sole heir, I wouldn't be able to discuss it with you at all."

"But you just said that I am."

"And so you are, sir. Do you know what a frag *pot* is, by the way?"

"I know what it was in Vietnam. Charlie told me."

"Enlighten me, if you would."

"Basically, it was a pile of money to pay for an assassination. Usually it was kept in an extra helmet, which is where the name 'pot' came in, but it could have been kept anywhere. When some troop had an officer who was really despised, they would start the collection. And every time the guy pissed somebody off again, a little more cash would get thrown in. When the pile was finally big enough to be worth risking a prison sentence, somebody would waste the officer in question and collect the reward. The preferred method of killing was with a grenade or a mine, which would leave no fingerprints or ballistic evidence."

"Aha. A fragmentary weapon, and hence the word 'frag,'" said Mildorf, nodding.

"I believe the word you want is 'fragmentation.'"

"Just so. Mr. Victor assumed I already knew all that, which made him a little hard to follow at times. Tell me, do you think this practice actually did happen?"

"Some people say it was really quite common, especially toward the end of the war, when the morale was all in the toilet."

"Well, then, maybe the box is believable, too, who knows? Mr. Victor claimed to have a box in which he was accumulating money to buy a political assassination."

"Really? Did he say who the target was?"

"He did not. And since it involved a criminal activity, I didn't ask."

"But whomever it was for, now the money is all mine."

"Exactly so."

"But only if I can find it."

"Correct again. I think there were supposed to be some instructions to you in the box, as well. As his executor, it would be up to me to enforce them. But since I cannot ethically enforce an illegal behest, and since I don't have the box anyway, I think it's safe to say all that is moot. Unless, of course, you already have the box?"

He took a large drink of his beer, which immediately reappeared as sweat on his forehead and cheeks. He took a tissue out of a back pocket and mopped at his brow. But through it all, he kept his eyes on me. If he was looking for a "tell," I disappointed him utterly. Then his hamburgers arrived, he paid Lefty, and nothing else could compete for his attention for a while.

"I don't suppose you have any idea why Charlie didn't tell me all this himself?"

With his mouth full of hamburger and onions, he nodded absently, then looked around and held both hands up with greasy fingers spread. I handed him a napkin, and he wiped first his hands and then his mouth before he spoke.

"Thank you. He might have wanted to, but he was trying to stay out of sight, as it were. When he came to see me, he snuck in the back way, through the fire escape stairs."

"That's not like him."

"If you say so, I believe you. But when I met him he was definitely running scared."

"Do you know of what?"

"I think he knew he was about to be murdered."

"Did he say that?"

"In a roundabout way. He found it ironic. He said, as I recall, 'After all these years, somebody is keeping a frag pot on me.' And then he used one of those colorful expressions I can never seem to remember. Something about a card."

"A death card, maybe?"

"Yes, that's it. Thank you. He said somebody had a death card for him. Or he himself had one; I don't remember which. Does that mean anything to you?"

"The ace of spades," I said. "Usually from a deck of cards with a military unit insignia on the back. Have you told the police any of this?"

"I have told you, Mr. Jackson. My legal duty is now discharged."

He gulped down the rest of his food and beer, stood, belched in a most undignified way, and started to leave.

"Stay a second," I said. "What about Charlie's body?"

"I'll play your ridiculous game. What about it?"

"What happens to it? Do I need to make some kind of arrangements?"

"You are the heir, not the next of kin. If you made some kind of arrangements, I'm sure nobody would argue with you. But you don't have to do anything. I assume they will keep the body for evidence for a while and then do whatever they do with homeless dead people."

"Which is what?"

"I have absolutely no idea."

He turned to go again, and this time, I let him. He did not look back at me, but he continued to cast hunted looks everywhere else.

I watched him leave, and wondered what, if anything, I should do about him. Even more, I wondered what I should do about Charlie's body. I hoped they wouldn't burn it. Then I remembered the will.

I pulled the papers out of my pocket and unfolded them. The first page seemed to be all preamble, with Mildorf's business address and Charlie's military service number, which was all he had in the way of ID. There were a lot of wheretofores and inasmuchas-es and *ipso factotums* that finally got us to the second page, where the real meat was. Once you got to it, it took only about half a page more for Charlie to call himself sane and me his heir. His scrawling signature, in real lawyers' blue ink, took up half of the remaining space, leaving a couple inches at the bottom that had something else written on it.

Printed in block letters, all caps, in pencil, it said simply, "YOU ARE BEING WATCHED." If it was true, it was definitely too bad, because somewhere out there was a box that might just contain thirty thousand dollars. And I rather badly needed twenty-five.

I decided I had hit enough pool balls for one day.

Fox and Geese

As I stepped out of the door from Lefty's, I scanned the sidewalk and the parked cars for a tail, but I couldn't spot one. But then, if it was any good, I wouldn't, would I? In a standard cougars-and-rabbits operation, there would be at least four shadows, two on each side of the street. Of course there was also the distinct possibility that G. Harold Mildorf was a babbling lunatic, which would also mean that I wouldn't spot a tail, because there wouldn't be one. But my gut instinct was that G. Harold was correct. And at some other level, I think I wanted him to be. Maybe I had acquired a will in more ways than one. It was time to engage the enemy.

I paused in front of Lefty's a bit longer, to let a couple of young black women pass in front of me. One was tiny and fragile-looking and incredibly pretty. From her size alone, I would have said she wasn't yet a teenager, but she had an air of quiet sorrow and dignity about her that made her look much older. She was pushing a baby stroller. Her friend was bigger, and there was nothing either pretty or quiet about her. She was also pushing a stroller, walking with something between a waddle and a swagger, gesturing wildly, and running her mouth non-stop. Since they were going in my direction, I fell in about ten paces behind them. But I could have heard the big one from a block away.

"So I says to her, 'What you trippin' on me about, bitch? Cramped chickenhead like you ain't got no call to be dissin' me.

Shit, you ain't even got no call to live.' An' she couldn't think of nothin' to say to *that*. Humph!"

She looked over at the small woman with a flash of triumph in her eyes. But the other one made no reply of any kind. She simply continued to look down and push her stroller at a slow, deliberate pace.

Getting no reaction, the big one decided to try again, with a slightly amped-up script.

"So I says to her, 'You better back off, bitch. You think you so phat, but I munna take you…'"

I decided that ten paces hadn't been nearly far enough. I stopped and took out a cigarette that I didn't really want and took my time lighting it, as if I couldn't concentrate on such a complicated task and walk at the same time. The stroller pushers were going awfully slowly, but I was determined to stall around long enough to let them get at least a half a block ahead of me.

That was when I spotted the first one.

Across the street and a little behind me, a tallish, nondescript guy in a dark nylon windbreaker and a mad bomber hat was suddenly taking a great interest in a storefront window. Innocuous enough, except the particular glass he was looking into belonged to a store that had been out of business for some three or four years. Now the place was used to store furniture that had never been taken out of its shipping cartons.

If they were running a classic box, Mr. Windbreaker's partner would be on my side of the street, maybe a half a block back. I looked back that way and saw a medium-height man in a crumpled raincoat walking away from me. He hadn't come out of Lefty's, or I would have noticed him there. And there weren't any other businesses in that block. Cougar number two. Three and four would be another half a block back.

I stayed where I was and smoked for a while, making no attempt to hide the fact that I was looking at the guy across the street. He kept his back to me, facing the glass, hands in pockets, pretending to be interested in the unremarkable display of boxes and dust. When I turned and headed east, back toward Lefty's, he seemed to hesitate for a moment. Then he, too, headed east. Ten seconds later, I looked at my watch, put on a phony expression of dismay, and did an abrupt one-eighty, once again heading west.

My man on the other side of the street suddenly had an overwhelming need to make a call on his cell phone. I thought I could pretty well imagine the content.

I think I might have been made.

Then you have been, idiot. Get out of there.

Of course, it was also possible that I was supposed to make him. They might let me have a glimpse of the scrubs, just so I wouldn't look too hard for the A-squad. That's assuming that I was worth a multiple-person surveillance team in the first place. If so, then my stock had gone up dramatically since I became the heir to a phantom estate and a cardboard box in some unknown location, a box that might have also been a frag pot.

I suppose I should have been flattered. I hadn't been the subject of that kind of interest since my Uncle Fred was being investigated by the feds for some trumped-up RICO charge. I was one of his collectors back then, so I got watched a lot by shadows that were ludicrously easy to spot. Back then, the FBI agents, even when they were working undercover, were strictly required to be clean shaven and wear a coat and tie at all times. But none of them made enough money to buy anything but off-the-rack suits and imitation silk ties. J. C. Penney's spies. I thought they were adorable.

I dressed better than any of them. In my early twenties, I thought of myself as a young professional, even though the job sometimes required more muscle than polish. I wore tailored wool-blend suits and button-down shirts made of the new permanent-press cotton blends. I preferred the wide ties that were popular then, but I wore narrow pineapple-knits, just to needle the feebes. I knew they weren't allowed to have them, because Mort Sahl, the comedian, always wore one. J. Edgar Hoover thought Sahl was a communist, and he hated him.

Fred's numbers and bets always came to him by phone, but the money came to about two dozen collection points around the city, mostly in bars, corner groceries, and laundries. I made the rounds several times a week. Any time I accumulated more than about three hundred dollars, I would feed it into a hidden box that I had welded behind the dash of my '72 Barracuda. It started its life as the housing for a defroster blower, so even if you stood on your head to get a look back there, it looked as if it belonged. If anybody ever demanded to know why I had $300 cash in my pocket, I would say I was going to buy a car from a friend. If they had been smart, they would have put some pressure on me by threatening to arrest me for failure to register for the draft, which was a federal misdemeanor. They had me there. The draft officially ended in 1973, but you were still legally required to register. But the feebes were never anything resembling smart. When Uncle Fred eventually went away for bookmaking, it was an undercover unit of the Detroit PD that nailed him. They weren't hampered by cheap suits.

Things were easier back then. Back then, it was a game. Now, my anonymity and maybe even my freedom were starting to feel a bit fragile, and it was not a good feeling at all.

Ahead of me, the so-I-tole-that-bitch monologue was still in full boom, though the extra distance helped a little.

"She so full of shit, I don't even mess with her. I just slap her right in the face."

Again, no reaction from the small, sad woman.

"That's what I do, all right. I slap her right in the face, knock her down, one time. She couldn't believe *that* shit. And then I says, 'Listen, bitch…'"

They stopped for a red light at Cedar Street, and I turned and walked south, leaving them behind me. I had no doubt that the loud one would keep retelling her story until Ms. Sad Eyes either became suitably impressed or told her she was full of shit. I was betting on her doing neither, and I wondered how many more times the routine would be replayed and how much more it would escalate. In half a block, it had gone from a story

of mere bad-mouthing to one of physical violence. In another few blocks, it could well be up to murder.

Somewhere once I read the number of times we can tell the same lie before we start to believe it ourselves. It was rather shockingly small. Something less than thirty. That probably meant that by this time tomorrow, the motor mouth would seriously believe she had assaulted somebody. That's if the offending other person even existed.

And maybe that didn't even matter.

That got me thinking about Charlie. He had decades to tell his stories. By the time I heard them, did they have anything at all to do with reality? Would he even know?

I thought about the day I first met Charlie Victor a little more than four years earlier. He had come into my office to ask about a bail bond, even though he was obviously not under arrest at the time.

Jackson Bail Bonds is the totally unglamorous name on my storefront, picked because "Herman Jackson, Bail Bonds" would have been just as unglamorous, as well as longer. But that's who I am and what I do. The sign is unilluminated, some would say just like its owner, and painted in a lettering style that the sign company called "Railroad Gothic." I think I liked the name more than the appearance. It called up images of wizened, colorful hobos with bizarre stories to tell. Under the main sign is a smaller one, in red neon, that says "24 Hour Service," with a phone number to call when the office is closed. Agnes says that's my lighthouse beacon, competing with the blue-lit crucifix of the Souls Harbor Mission over in the wino district north of Lowertown, for the traffic of souls lost in the night. That's what she says, that is, when she isn't complaining about the fact that the 24/7 service means she has no social life whatsoever. I never did have one, so I don't worry about it.

Charlie walked in during regular business hours and said, simply, "What's it cost for a bond?"

"For a friend?"

"No, man, for me."

"What did you do?" I said.

"When?" He looked behind him, as if there might be a train wreck in the street that he hadn't noticed, one that he might be blamed for.

"When you did whatever you did that you need a bond for."

"If I'd already done it, I couldn't be here now, could I? I mean, I'd be under arrest, wouldn't I?" He looked at me as if he were talking to a total idiot.

"That would be a problem," I said, "yes."

"Well, there you are, then," he said. "I ain't done nothing yet. I want to know what it costs first."

And they say there's nothing new under the ancient sun.

"Let me get this straight," I said. "You're contemplating doing some kind of crime, but first you want to know what the bail will be if you get caught?"

"Oh, I'll get caught, all right. I don't know how to do much, but I know how to get caught, all to hell. I wouldn't waste your time, otherwise."

"Of course not." And there I was, indeed.

I motioned him to my classic Motel Six lobby chair, even though Agnes shot me a look that clearly said, "Don't you dare!" She gets a little nervous when we have clients who look as color- ful as they really are.

Bonding is a funny business, and in some ways, she has never gotten used to it. Bonding is safe, is the thing to remember. In a system that is full of attitude and even rage, people almost never get mad at the bondsman. It's a little like being a ringside doctor in a prizefight where lethal weapons are allowed. The fight stops momentarily, you assess the damages and do what you can about them, and then the bell rings and the chaos starts all over again. A lot of the customers don't even remember you.

I once had a guy in my office, in cuffs and leg irons, who tried to attack the cop who was escorting him. He used his feet and teeth and head, but he mostly just managed to get the living crap beat out of him. But he never made a move of any kind

toward me. When it was all over, the cop was kneeling on the guy's back with a nightstick jammed down on his neck.

"You gonna bond this guy?" he asked.

"That's a trick question, right? A sobriety test?"

"I got to hear it officially," said the cop.

"No, I'm not going to bond him. Is that official enough?"

"Perfect." He jerked the man, who was still officially only a suspect, to his feet and bopped him once more on the ear, just for punctuation. Then he hustled him out, ignoring a sputtering tirade about police brutality.

"You don't know who you're fucking with, pig." The man was screaming, despite split lips and missing teeth. "Someday I'm gonna get out, and I'll find you and spill your blood and wipe your woman's face in it. And then I'll start on her." Then he turned to me, and in a completely calm voice said, "Sorry about the mess on the carpet, man."

"Hey, no problem," I said. He was a suspect, all right. At least, I sure as hell suspected him.

Anyway, Agnes watched the whole scene in appalled silence, and since then, she keeps a .38 revolver in her desk. As far as I know, she has never fired it, and I have never made it an issue.

I managed to look somewhere else as Agnes eased open the drawer where she kept her heat. Then I offered our possible new client a cup of coffee.

He took a look at the carafe on the table in the corner and said, "You got to be kidding."

"Some people are happy to get it," I said. I mean, gee, it wasn't all *that* old.

"Some people are happy to get a shot of radiator juice," he said, "but that don't make it bottled in bond. What do I look like, a goddamn bum?"

I looked him over before I replied. He had a wedge-shaped face that was too large for the rest of his body, and he made a lot of sudden, jerky motions with it, like a cat who's been out on the streets too long and can't ever relax. It was hard to tell with all the rags he wore, but I thought he must have had a powerful frame and broad shoulders once. Now he had a permanent stoop and one hand that was curled with arthritis, though he still carried himself with a certain stubborn dignity. Ex-military, I decided. Maybe that unit patch on his old fatigue jacket was real, at that. There was something else, too, some quality that made me think that he was down but definitely not out.

"Actually," I said, "you look more like a hobo."

"A connoisseur," he snorted. "I come in to ask about the cost of a bond, and I get a goddamn connoisseur of untouchables. A gourmet of street people."

"I used to be," I said, "but it's harder to tell them apart nowadays."

"Yeah? Well, I'll help you out. I used to be a stockbroker, okay? Had friends in high places, money in low ones, and prospects up the wazoo. But I got sick of all that crap, and I dropped out of the system to give all my time to helping the oppressed, legalizing pot, and freeing Tibet."

I had no idea what kind of response that was meant to evoke, so I gave him none. After I had looked blank for half a minute, he spoke again, this time with a lot less energy.

"That was a joke," he said. His shoulders suddenly sagged even farther, and his face fell. His mind had switched to a different channel.

"Oh," I said.

"About lost causes, see."

"I see. And you're into lost causes? Or is that the joke?"

"You shitting me? I *am* a lost cause, son. I been down so long, it looks like up to me."

This time I laughed, and so did he. And for reasons I couldn't begin to explain, I knew I was going to like the guy.

"So tell me about this crime you're planning on getting caught for," I said.

"Well, I haven't picked one yet. I mean, you got to see what opportunities come your way. And you gotta be careful, too. Purse snatching is good, but if you pick some hyper old broad with gardening of the hearteries, say, she can get a stroke or a heart attack, and all of a sudden, it's murder. And breaking and entering is okay, but if you pick a place that's got too much money inside, that can turn into big-time hard time, too. What you want is some nice little felony misdemeanor that will get you ninety or a hundred in the County workhouse, and no hard feelings. Smashing a window on a cop car is all right, as long as you make sure there's no damn dog behind it, but sometimes—"

"Are you telling me…"

"Winter's coming on, Harold."

"It's Herman."

"No, it's fall. And pretty soon, my cardboard box down under the wye-duct just ain't gonna cut it anymore."

"I think it's time to brush up on your O. Henry," said Agnes from her keyboard.

Good grief, was that really what this was all about? Were we about to play out "The Cop and the Anthem," about the bum trying to get thrown in jail for the winter? If so, I was sure it would be without the surprise epiphany at the end.

"What's a wye-duct?" I said.

"It's like a bridge," he said, "only not over a river. It goes over some train tracks or a road or something. You know, like in the old song: 'Oh, I live under the wye-duct; Down by the winny-gar woiks.'"

"Oh, that old song." Huh? Where the hell was he from, anyway, an old black-and-white movie? "So you're looking to get locked up someplace warm for the winter?"

"The County Workhouse," said Charlie, nodding vigorously and looking suddenly gleeful. Another channel switch. "Not just someplace. And for sure not the damn jail."

"Then why do you need a bond?"

"So I don't gotta sit in *jail* while I wait for my hearing to come up so I can get my sentence and go to the *workhouse*."

"So instead, you sit in your box and freeze?" I said.

"Life's a bitch, Howard."

"Herman."

"Him, too. See, the timing is everything. Just like in war. You ever been in combat?"

"No." At least, that's not what it was called. In the part of Detroit where I grew up, the streets were never exactly peaceful, except when the night people were asleep and the working stiffs were off at their jobs. Or maybe when there was a free barbeque at the UAW hall. So I knew a bit about timing, but I still didn't get why he wanted the bond. "What's so bad about sitting in jail for a week or so?"

He gave me a pained look, then spoke slowly and carefully, as if it were explaining a difficult topic to a retarded child. He tapped his finger on my coffee table to empathize each syllable.

"Jail," he said, tapping and then pointing to the brick building a little over a block away, "is not like the workhouse." Tappity-*tap*. "Jail is full of *crazy* people!" Big bunch of taps. "You can get *hurt* in there."

I had absolutely no argument for that.

Since he might actually be about to become a paying customer, and also just because he seemed to need it, I walked him over to the Gopher Bar and Grill on Wacouta and bought him lunch. We had Coney Islands, the house specialty, and mugs of draft beer, and after a few follow-up beers plus a shot or two to cut the bubbles, he got that faraway, changing-channels look again, and we both traveled back to the jungle on the other side of the world.

In Country

South Vietnam
1965

On Charlie's first night in country, he was put with a company on perimeter night-guard duty at an artillery firebase. They manned a string of two- and three-man foxholes fifty yards outside their own concertina wire, well into the fringe of the bush. Their orders were simple. "If you see any VC trying to sneak up with sapper charges, kill them."

The catch was that they couldn't see anything at all.

Nobody had any night vision goggles or even any flares, except for one of the sergeants, who had a sniper rifle with a starlight scope. A few grunts had brought flashlights, but they didn't dare turn them on, for fear of drawing fire. And the jungle in front of them was as black as only true wilderness can be.

Their only other order was that no matter what happened, they were not to leave their foxholes.

Charlie was in a sandbagged foxhole with a goofy kid from some wide spot in the road in Georgia and a big black guy from some ghetto in Washington, D.C. The kid was named Junior Sauer, and the black guy called himself Bong. Charlie thought they were either screw-ups or nut cases. But even so, they knew the territory and the drill, and he didn't.

"This is a bullshit detail, man," said Sauer.

"Uh huh," said Bong. "What you think they put us on it for? We get overrun, it don't matter, because the firebase is all safe back behind us yet. But we get attacked and kill some gooks instead, then the lieut back in the hooch gets a nice little pat on his West Point ass for upping his body count. So he puts nothing out here but fuckups and FNGs, dig? Which one are you?" He gave Charlie a gentle poke.

"What's an FNG?" said Charlie.

"Fucking new guy. What I tell you, Junior? Nothing out here but us disposables."

"Well, it's still bullshit. Hey new guy, you carrying anything?"

"Am I carrying anything? Are you serious? I think I'm carrying every damn piece of gear the Army ever bought."

"Jesus, Bong, was we ever that new?"

The big man laughed. To Charlie he said, "He's talking about dew, Man. Something to get high on. Some Mary Joanna or some uppers or something."

"You can't get high on guard, for chrissake."

"Sure you can. Sarge don't care. You watch; he'll be one of the first ones firing up a joint. Acid's no good, though. Guys on that stuff do crazy shit, like try to fly or go playing around with grenades. You try dropping any acid, I'll kick your ass."

Charlie decided he had just been thrown into the snake pit, with the unfortunate handicap of being sane.

Then the last sliver of red-orange sun slipped over the horizon, and faster than he could have believed, blackness slammed down on them like the lid of God's coffin.

The entire world disappeared.

Charlie literally couldn't see his hand in front of his face. He couldn't even tell which way was up, which gave him a sense of falling. His face felt hot and prickly and he suddenly found that he had trouble catching his breath. He was glad he didn't have to run anywhere, because he was sure his legs wouldn't work any more.

"Hey new guy, where you from?"

"The Iron R..., um, Minnesota."

"The Iron Rum-in-a-soda. Never heard of that place, did you, Junior?"

"No way, Bong. They got dark like this in Rum-in-a-soda?"

"Sure. Um, ah, no. I don't know. Down in the mines, maybe. Is it always like this?"

"No, man, sometimes it gets real dark, you know?"

He could hear Junior giggling, and it should have pissed him off, he knew, but he just didn't care. So much for all the bullshit about brothers-in-arms that they fed him in Basic.

Basic.

In Basic, the targets were all exactly fifty or a hundred yards away. In Basic, you could always see the targets, and they didn't shoot back. And in Basic, the people around you were dependable, and if they didn't know what they were doing, the sergeant did.

Basic was Fantasyland.

He didn't know what this place was.

Then the big 155-millimeter long toms ripped open the night with their thunder. The ground trembled, and multiple shock waves and flashes of yellow-white strobe light came from behind the foxholes. Somewhere, miles away, some forward patrol had called for artillery support, and the firebase was pouring it out.

Charlie looked at the jungle in front of him in flashbulb blinks. Had it looked like that in the daylight? Were there new shapes there now, advancing between glimpses, hiding, coming to kill him? He hugged his M16, pressed the barrel against his cheek and smelled the oil. Had he used enough? Metal corroded in the jungle, he had heard, while you were still putting away the cleaning rag. And corroded M-16s jammed, were already famous for jamming. Hell, they would jam if you gave them a dirty look.

He wanted to cry.

He wanted to be very, very small.

He wanted to die.

No, that was wrong, check that thought. He wanted to live, but he wanted to quit being so very afraid. Hell, he didn't know what he wanted, except that he wanted to be anywhere at all except where he was. And he hated the goddamned Army.

Then, as suddenly as they had opened up, the big guns fell silent, and all he could hear was the rock music. Jesus H. fucking Christ, some idiot had turned on a boom box!

"Is everybody here completely nuts?" said Charlie.

"Shit, man," said Junior Sauer, "that's what this war's all about. Make the world safe for rock and roll, y'all. Ain't no other reason to be here."

"Yeah, but—"

"What's it matter, anyhow?" said Bong, somewhere in the darkness. "You think Charlie don't know where we are, after that salvo? He damn sure got us all zeroed in now."

They heard a rifle shot from off to their left, and the radio died. Charlie figured the sergeant with the night scope had shot it. Whether that was true or not, it touched off a hailstorm of fire up and down the line. Red tracers from the company's three heavy machine guns went streaming off into the jungle, and the chorus of rifle and pistol fire around them became deafening. Now and then, somebody tossed a grenade into the bush, just to up the ante. People were screaming as they fired, some of them standing up in their foxholes.

Charlie didn't know what to do.

"Fire your weapon, man!"

"At what? I can't see a damn thing."

"It don't matter. We put enough lead out there, won't nothin' get past it. Hell, we'll kill the fuckin' bugs."

"But we don't have—"

"Will you goddamnit fire your fucking weapon?"

So Charlie fired his M-16. He fired until his magazine was empty and then he locked in another one and kept firing, caught up in the blind frenzy that was sweeping through the company.

And he found that as stupid as it was, frenzy was better than fear.

After a few minutes, a sergeant came by and tapped them each on the forearm and shouted at them to cease firing. And they did so, for just about as long as it took for the sergeant to move on to the next hole. Then the shooting started again, as furiously as ever.

Eventually they ran out of ammunition.

Up and down the line, the foxholes fell silent. And as the frenzy died out, soldiers checked their luminous-faced watches and realized they still had almost six hours of watch left to stand, with no ammunition. They fixed their bayonets, stared intently into the dark, and didn't speak.

It was the longest night of Charlie's life.

The next day, the tension dissipated with the first morning light, replaced by a mind-numbing fatigue and a vague sense of shame. They straggled back through the wire, to where the lieutenant who commanded the company was waiting for them, hands on hips, jungle cammos flawlessly cleaned and pressed, jump boots gleaming like patent leather. His mouth was a single, stern slash, his eyes inscrutable behind dark aviator glasses. As they shuffled past him, he returned their salutes with exaggerated crispness.

Charlie couldn't remember how close he was supposed to get before he saluted, and he probably waited too long. Thus, he committed the Army's most unforgivable mistake: he let himself be noticed by an officer.

"Stand fast, Private!"

"Yes, sir."

"You don't say 'yes sir' to that order, shithead, you just do it. Why aren't you holding your salute?"

"Well, you said—"

"I said stand fast. I did not say fuck off."

Charlie added a frozen salute to his braced posture and thought about how much he hated the Army. The lieutenant did not return his salute.

"Did you learn anything last night, Private?"

What could he say to that without getting into trouble?

"Sir, yes sir."

"All you men stand fast! Private Shithead here is going to tell us what he learned from your pathetic little mad-moment fireworks binge last night."

Jesus, he just wasn't going to let it go, was he?

"Let's hear it, Private. Loud and clear."

And before he had time to think about what he was doing, the words came tumbling out of his mouth like heretical lemmings, gleefully bound for self-destruction.

"Sir, I learned that there is a great lack of leadership and direction in the field. Sir."

And that was how Charlie came to be designated as the company's replacement tunnel-rat.

<>‹›‹›

He survived as a tunnel rat for over nine months, which was long enough to get a betting pool started on the date of his eventual death. Short-timers always bet on tomorrow or the day after, but more and more, the smart money was saying that he might actually survive his tour of duty.

In a country full of ways to die, clearing the VC tunnels was notable for being one of the worst. If you ran into an AK-47 round or a poisoned punjii stick or one of those hard-to-see, blink-quick, deadly little green snakes that were everywhere, it was an open question whether or not anybody else in your unit would even go down after you and pull out your body.

But as he survived more and more descents, Charlie started to get deadly, too.

He learned to hear and even sense bodies in the pitch dark and he learned when to pursue and waste and when to retreat or hide. He found that if he plugged his ears up with huge wads of chewing gum, he could drop grenades into lower, intersecting tunnels without giving himself a concussion. He learned to shoot by feel, in places so dark that he couldn't see the sights on his guns.

He acquired a pair of .45 pistols, called John Wayne rifles, a seven-shot .38 revolver, and a long machete that he filed down to make into a sort of double-edged sword. He also got a three-foot-long bamboo stick that he taped an extra flashlight to, so he could light the tunnel ahead without giving away his true location.

The gear gave him confidence, and the confidence gave him time. Time to learn how to be invisible and time to learn to kill. He learned to kill in very confined quarters, at very close range. He learned to kill without hesitation or remorse or even thought. He began to be famous. He was known as Chazbo the Tunnel King.

He was a great disappointment to Lt. Rappolt.

Then one day his company abandoned him.

<>·<>·<>

It was a high profile, supposedly high-percentage operation, with reporters and TV cameras. Three full companies were choppered into the bush around a ville that I-Corps was sure was a VC sanctuary, if not an actual stronghold. The plan was to surround the ville on three sides, kill off the VC who stood and fought, and drive the rest of them off into a low mountain pass, where another two airborne companies waited in ambush.

It was textbook air-mobile tactics. It was guaranteed to work. Officers like Rappolt actually accompanied their own troops, though not in the first wave of choppers. It was a photo op for an officer on the way up.

And it was "fugazi" from the get-go, the Nam-era name for SNAFU.

For openers, the place was abandoned. There was nobody there but a few chickens and pigs, who seemed to mock the American troops as smugly as did the empty huts.

There were a few baskets of rice and other foodstuffs, and when the grunts kicked them over, they blew up. There were also a few weapons, which they didn't touch. And there were a few tunnel entrances. Rappolt let himself be photographed dropping a grenade into one of them. Then he sent the photographers away and sent for Charlie.

Charlie waited a few minutes for the smoke to clear, dumped all but his essential killing gear, and dropped into the biggest and most complicated underground maze he had yet been in. After he passed three branching points, he backtracked to the beginning and started all over again, this time spreading a trail of baking soda behind him. He had learned that baking soda worked better than a string, which the enemy could move.

He found a lot of shafts leading back up to more entrances into the village. He found two large galleries where troops had probably slept and an electrically lit medical dressing station. From there, a string of bare light bulbs lit a long tunnel in a direction he thought was back into the mountains. He jerked on a wire from one of the bulbs, and far down the tunnel, something exploded and took all the lights out with it.

He turned his flashlight back on and followed the trail of white powder back the way he had come. To press farther ahead was practically asking to trip another booby trap or walk into an ambush.

Twice on the way back, he thought he heard a sound coming from a cross-gallery, and he emptied his .45s into the opening as he passed it.

When he finally came back out into the daylight, he looked at his watch and was surprised to see that he had been underground for almost two hours.

And his entire company was gone.

He ran through the ville, first in disbelief and then with a rising feeling of pure panic. It couldn't be. Not even the dead were totally abandoned, unless the company was under such intense attack that it was impossible to take them out. But there was no sign of any battle here at all. No shell casings, no burning huts, no smell of cordite or HE in the air. His people had simply flown away and left him down in the tunnels.

But they had left a radio.

He found it not far from the first tunnel hatch, and a little red light and some static seemed to say that it was operational. He keyed the SEND button and spoke, surprised to find that his panic was now almost totally replaced by anger.

"This is Private Charles Victor, Golf Company. You guys left me, over."

When the handset had nothing to say in reply, he tried again, this time forcing himself to remember to release the sending button after he talked. He got an immediate response.

"What's your radio code, soldier?"

"How the hell should I know? I'm not a radioman; I'm the guy you left behind, okay? Over!"

"That's a negative on swearing over the air, private. Try again, with the code for the day, and this time, tell us where you are. Over."

"I'm wherever Golf got choppered today, where do you think I am?"

"That would be a classified location, over." The voice continued to be infuriatingly calm.

"Well of course it is, you dumb fuck! I didn't ask you to broadcast it, I just want you to come back and get me. The sun goes down here, this place is going to be nothing but void vicious."

"You were told not to use profanity on the airwaves, private. And if you have no radio code and no location, there's no way we can..."

"What kind of dumbfuck tripwire vet am I talking to? GET ME THE HELL OUT OF HERE!"

"You are talking to Lieutenant Rappolt, soldier, and you're either an imposter or somebody way out of line. Either way, without a code, you're SOL. Over. And. Out."

Charlie shouted every obscenity and swear word he knew into the radio. Then he threw it on the ground and kicked it several times. Then he shot it. Finally he hunkered down on the ground and wept.

And when he had wept long enough, he picked up his gear and walked into the jungle.

Faux Box

My shadows had managed to become invisible now, but I was sure they would still be with me. *Maybe I should write Charlie an obit*, I thought, and I smiled at the reaction that would have gotten from him. And then I did a mental double take and thought maybe that was exactly what I should do. In a way, anyway. First, though, I wanted to set up a little street theatre.

I headed up the Fourth Street hill and back toward my office, but I went on past it and then across the street and down the block to Nickel Pete Carchetti's pawnshop. Its name is Pawn USA, but I always call it the Emporium of Broken Dreams.

An old-fashioned jingle bell clanked as I went in the door and saw Pete brooding at his usual perch behind the teller's cage. With a jeweler's loupe stuck on his troll-like forehead, he looked like one of the seven dwarfs, just back from the mines. Grumpy, to be exact. His bottle of Pepto-Bismol was on the counter in front of him, half full, and I guessed his Panzer-class heartburn was staging another major offensive.

"Herman, old friend." He raised his chin by way of greeting and gave me his idea of a smile. Then he took a swig of his pink elixir. "All by yourself, for a change, instead of bringing me one of your sleazy clients with some piece of junk to hock. I feel honored. No doubt you came to take me out to lunch."

"After you called my customers sleazy?"

"Well what do you call them, pillars of society?"

"Pillagers, more often. But you're not exactly in the carriage trade, either, you know."

"Hmm. No, I guess not. I had a great-grandfather who was, sort of, but they called it something different back then." He sighed, spread his hands on the counter, and stared up at some invisible object to his left.

"Like robbing trains?"

"Stagecoaches."

"Much more elegant. I need a cigar box."

"Excuse me?" His eyes snapped back down and refocused, and he looked a little pissed that I had interrupted his reverie.

"You know, one of those little wood things with phony brass hinges and circus graphics on the lid? I think cigars used to come in them once, though I can't honestly say I've ever seen any."

"I know what a cigar box is, Herman. I'm an educated man. What I don't know is why you would come to me for one. Try maybe an antique store. Hell, try a cigar store. I'm not in the box business."

"I will make no comment on what kind of business you're in, Pete. Do you have one or not?"

"I might could find one. Mind telling me what you want it for?"

"It's kind of a long story."

"So give me the made-for-TV version."

"Okay, the short take is this: it's possible that I'm being followed right now. If that's true, I want my shadow to see me come out of a pawn shop carrying a ratty-looking old box that you just might have been holding for me."

"That all sounds very B-movie-ish. Which by the way, I got a good assortment of. I even got Beta."

"Beta is deader than Elvis, Pete."

"No it's not. It's good stuff, always was. I got the players, too, is the thing. Give you just a hell of a deal on a whole package."

"We were talking about boxes, I believe."

"Yeah, yeah, all right then." This time he gave me his Oscar-quality sigh. "You care if anything is in this box?"

"It might actually be better if there is."

"How about a pasteboard item that's held together by a couple of big rubber bands and is full of some costume jewelry that's so crappy, even I can't peddle it?"

"Sounds perfect. Stick a phony claim ticket on it and it will be better yet."

"The things I do for you."

⟨⟩⟨⟩⟨⟩

The box turned out to be white, with a picture of a two-corona owl on the front, and it looked suitably junky and also light-colored enough to be seen from a good distance away. I borrowed a Magic Marker from Pete, peeled back the rubber band temporarily, and wrote:

CHARLIE VICTOR——HIS BOX
OPEN WITH CAUTION

I smiled at my handiwork and gave him back the marker. He didn't charge me for the box.

"But you realize, of course, that now you really do owe me a lunch?"

"Fair enough, Pete."

"Damn straight it is. Just don't make good on it until you lose your tail, whoever it is, okay? What I do not need in what's left of my wretched old life is a bunch of cloak and dagger shit, is what."

"Got it." I put the box conspicuously under my arm and headed back out into the crisp air. Time to visit the fourth estate.

⟨⟩⟨⟩⟨⟩

Three blocks later, I was back on Cedar, at the main office of the *Pioneer Press*. The place had a grand lobby at street level that actually contained nothing but a desk for receiving mail, a lot of photomurals, and a big spiral staircase that led up to the skyway level. There, a pretty receptionist at a tiny desk managed to look cheerful and sweet while she mostly told people to go away.

"I'd like to talk to a reporter, please."

"Do you have a news story for us, or are you concerned about one that we've already printed?"

"I'm concerned about one that you should have printed but didn't. I'd like to find out why."

"And what is your point of view, sir, if I may ask?"

"I was a witness." What a nice way of asking me if I'm a nut case with an axe to grind. I gave her what I hoped was a bland smile, just to show her I wasn't dangerous.

"A witness to…?"

"A fire." *That's good, Jackson. Keep it simple. Stay away from the conspiracy-theory stuff.*

"You mean like a house fire?"

"More like an area fire, down in Connemara Gulch."

"Like a brush fire, you mean? I don't think we—"

"Not brush. Something directed at homeless people. Somebody was deliberately torching their campsites."

"I think you should be talking to the police, sir."

I just never seem to listen to my own advice.

She began punching buttons on her console, but not 911, I noticed. Their own security, more likely. I was obviously making the poor young woman feel threatened. Now she was sending for the people with the white coats and truncheons.

"In fact, sir, I can…" She ran her free hand through her hair, frowned once, hung up her receiver, picked it up again and punched some different buttons.

"I'll talk to this gentleman, Pam." The unexpected voice of calm came from a petite, dark-haired woman with a perfectly tailored suit and a bemused look. She had come out of the passing skyway pedestrian traffic, coat folded over one arm and thin leather gloves in her other hand. The receptionist named Pam looked surprised and relieved, and she gave the newcomer a palms-up gesture that said, "your funeral."

"I'm Anne Packard," she said, shifting her coat to her left arm so she could offer me her hand.

"Herman Jackson. Pleased to meet you."

"Herman Jackson the bail bondsman?" Her grip was surprisingly strong for a woman's, and she held it longer than I expected. I looked at her face again and saw alert and probing eyes that had little laugh creases at the corners, a sharp nose, and thin, not-quite-smiling lips. She reminded me of a psychotherapist I once knew: very pleasant to chat with, but you wanted to be damn careful what you said to her. And she already knew who I was, which was more than a bit jarring.

"I'm impressed," I said. "I didn't realize I was known to the press."

"You should be impressed. It's part of being a reporter, and I work at it. I know the names of all the businesses that I pass regularly. Sooner or later, I will know all the faces and stories that go with them, too. You, however, have just missed your big chance to impress me. You're supposed to say, 'Oh, wow, Anne Packard! I read your column every day! Great stuff.'"

"Didn't I say that? I was sure I said that. I certainly thought it. I probably thought 'witty and incisive,' too."

"Nice try. Tell you what, though: buy me a cup of coffee at the little deli over there, and I'll listen to your story anyway."

"I was hoping for a real reporter. No offense."

"A *real* reporter? You mean instead of a *mere* columnist? Well, I was hoping for a *real* scoop from an unimpeachable source, and a *real* Pulitzer Prize for writing it. No offense. How about if we both take a chance here?"

"When you put it so charmingly, how could I refuse?"

"God, I hope your story is better than your pickup line."

Was that a pickup line? I hadn't thought so, but in any case, we walked over to a little hole-in-the-skyway C-store and mini-deli that had wrought iron chairs and tiny tables, right out in the pedestrian traffic across from Pam's desk. I got us two regular coffees in Styrofoam cups and we settled down to talk newspaper talk.

I told her all the parts of the previous night's events that didn't sound like lunatic raving. The very short version, in other words. I did not say anything about the kid with the snow shovel or my being followed.

"Between a murder right downtown and the fire in the Gulch, I thought at least one of the two stories would have found its way into your paper," I said.

"Don't be so disingenuous. You also think the two stories are related."

"Okay, you got me. I wouldn't have thought so, except that some street people over in Railroad Island told me a couple of federal agents were there last night, looking for the dead guy's squat."

"His what?"

"His nest, his patch, whatever you want to call it. The cardboard box he lived in."

She nodded her understanding, and I went on. "This morning, the same feds were in my office, looking for something they thought I was holding for him. Turns out, they're Secret Service."

"Are you sure they're the same agents?" She had started taking some notes on a miniature steno pad, which I took to be a positive sign.

"No. To be perfectly honest, I have no proof of that at all."

She looked up from her writing and gave me a very penetrating look and the tiniest hint of a smile, and I figured I had just passed some kind of credibility test.

"Drink some coffee," she said.

So I did.

While I tasted dark, too-hot coffee and plastic, she produced a cell phone and made three calls, taking a lot of notes and frequently furrowing her brows. I sat back in my chair and stared at the ceiling, making a show of not trying to hear her conversation.

Finally she put the phone back in its clip-on belt holster and once again stared thoughtfully into my eyes while she tapped the eraser end of her pencil on her note pad.

"Very curious," she said.

"What is?" If *she* was very curious, that could be very good for the home team.

"I have some good sources in Fire, Police, and the County Morgue," she said. "Nice folks, people who don't bullshit me or try to freeze me out."

"How handy for you."

"It usually is. Today, they're all sounding a bit on the phony side. And they're not even being very clever about it. The official story is that the fire was a brush fire, probably accidentally set by homeless people trying to keep warm."

"Brush doesn't usually burn very well in a snowstorm, does it?"

"I'm not sure. And the official story on your homeless guy is that he died of exposure."

"I agree. Exposure to brass knuckles, exposure to boots, exposure to some very nasty people. The question is, why are the cops trying to whitewash it?"

"Drink some more coffee." She dug her phone back out and made two more calls, taking still more notes. Then she scowled at her notes, tried some of her own coffee, and looked back up at me.

"Neither of your stories would have made the morning edition. Our usual deadline is four p.m. But my editor says we aren't running anything on them this afternoon, either. We're sitting on the death story as a courtesy to somebody who wants to see who comes poking their noses into it."

"Meaning me."

"I would say so. Interesting, though, how he doesn't say who the favor was for, and he also does not use the word 'murder' at all."

"But that would explain my visit from the Secret Service, wouldn't it?"

"It could explain why they picked you to visit," she said, "but not why they were interested in this dead person in the first place." She drank some more coffee and did some more scowling at her notes. "It's also interesting that my editor told me to forget about the whole business."

"Does it work, telling a reporter to do that?"

"You bet. It just about guarantees that I will investigate further. And it also allows him to deny he ever told me to."

"Neat. So now what happens?"

"That depends on how serious you are, Mr. Jackson."

"Me? Serious?"

"Serious enough to take a little walk with me?"

"To Connemara Gulch?"

She nodded. "Show me where you saw what you saw."

"Absolutely."

As she was getting her coat back on, I happened to look down at Pete's cigar box and get a sudden inspiration.

"Listen, this box is sort of heavy to lug around. Could I leave it with your receptionist, Pam, until we get back?"

"What's in it?"

"Just some low-grade client collateral." I hoped I said that loud enough for Pam to hear and remember.

"Sure, why not? Pam?"

"No problem, sir." She was, I'm sure, delighted to be rid of me so easily.

As Anne Packard and I set off down the skyway at a brisk pace, I noted the location of the security cameras in the reception area. I liked the setup.

"Ms. Packard—"

"Call me Anne."

"Anne, then. Do you by chance know anybody who can lift a fingerprint off a snow shovel?"

"Is that a trick question?"

Sheeny Gulch

My informants from the night before were nowhere to be seen as I led the way through the industrial debris at the rim of the Gulch. The snow was all melted now, leaving scores of little rivulets dribbling down toward the hollow and hundreds of puddles that weren't draining anywhere at all. I was glad I wasn't wearing any shoes that had cost more than sixteen-fifty at the outlet mall. Anne Packard's, I noticed, were much more sensible than mine, rugged-looking things that were almost like low hiking boots. I wondered if she kept a pair of classy-looking heels at her desk. Then I wondered what she looked like in them. I wondered a lot of things that I had no business thinking about at all.

"Are your street people, the ones you said saw the federal agents, still around?" she asked.

"I don't see them," I said. "And we're just as glad for that, since neither of us has a sidearm."

"A cell phone is better," she said. "Nobody attacks you if they can see you can call for help. You don't carry one, I take it?"

"I'd rather die."

"Well, it's good that you understand your options so clearly."

The road down into the gulch didn't look nearly as steep as I remembered it.

"This is where I watched it from," I said. "This gate was closed and had some burly type guarding it, but he left when the commotion started down below."

"And you didn't follow?"

"Nope, I chickened out, pure and simple."

"You obviously have no reporter's instincts."

"Also no unnatural desire to go in harm's way. I expect to die someday, but I'm really not ready for it just yet."

"Well, there are no flames now. Let's go see if they left any traces."

As we descended on the rutted gravel roadway, I began to feel more than a bit foolish. Things looked so ordinary in the daylight. What did I really expect to find, a ten-ton pile of ashes? Anne Packard led the way, and I saw her looking over her shoulder at me from time to time. I was sure she could read my mind.

Down in the trough of the gulch, there were several sets of train tracks, some rusted and some shiny from recent use, piles of old railroad ties, a lot of scrub brush, and all kinds of assorted rubbish. There was still some snow in the shaded areas under bushes or trees, but most of it was gone, leaving just wet stones and mud. A lot of the underbrush and the rubbish looked blackened, but the effects of mildew, random trash fires, and spilled creosote and oil were impossible to distinguish from what we were looking for. Now and then, Anne would poke at a black branch on a scrubby tree, to see if the soot on it was fresh. Then she would throw me a look that I was sure said, "You brought me here for *this?*"

I was rehearsing an apology when she pushed aside a burned head-high poplar, stopped, and said, "Oh my God."

"Something?" I said, rushing to catch up to her.

"Dog."

"Dog?"

"Dead dog," she said. "Burned. And look at the tracks in what's left of the snow."

I looked. It had been a big dog of some kind. Now it was a grotesque, blackened corpse, and it had left deep marks in the snow and dirt, as if it had tried to burrow into the earth to stop the fire, or at least the pain. And most telling of all, what was left of its fur still smoked faintly. I wanted to cry for it.

"What do you think?" she said.

"I'll tell you what I don't think. I don't think this dog died from a trash fire set by homeless people."

"No. Not from careless cigarette smoking, either." She pulled a tiny silver camera out of her purse and began weaving around, looking for a good angle. "Pity," she said. "I don't think we can print anything this heart-rending. Why would anybody do such a thing?"

"They was tryna make an example, is what."

We both turned around to see that the voice came from a shapeless, pasty-faced woman with about three scarves on her head, oversized rubber boots on her feet, and uncounted layers of clothes everywhere else.

"First they beat up on some of the guys, and when that didn't do no good, they started burnin'. They had cans of gas or somethin', an they burnt our stuff and then they burnt the dog, said they'd do the same to us. Poor thing screamed something awful. Finally they shot it."

"Who?" I said. "Who were they?"

"Who wants to know?"

"Press," said Anne, producing a business card and a winning smile faster than I would have believed possible.

"Strib?" said the bag lady, squinting at the card. "The good one?"

"*Pioneer Press*," I said. "The local one." Anne gave me a dirty look.

"Oh, that one."

"Tell us what these people wanted," said Anne, starting to shoot pictures of the woman.

"What's in it for me? You got some money for me?"

I started to reach for my wallet, but Anne pushed my hand down and said, "You'll get your picture in the paper. Maybe you'll even get quoted. Would you like that?"

"Really? Front page?"

"That's up to my editor. I'll do what I can."

"Will you bring me a copy?"

"Sure. Lots of copies."

"Will you tell everybody how I lost my job at the bank when I wouldn't fuck the manager?"

"Tell us about the people who killed the dog."

"I'd really like to see that asshole reported on. Bet his fat-assed wife and ugly kids don't even know—"

"The fire? Please try to stay on track, miss, um…?"

"Glenda." She furrowed her already wrinkled brows and nodded. "I think so. Yeah. I started hitting the juice just a little harder than I should a few weeks back, maybe, and sometimes I forget some stuff. But I'm pretty sure it's Glenda. Like the witch, you know? I don't s'pose you got any red? I remember real good with a shot of the red."

Swell, I thought. *My only corroborating witness, and she turns out to be a wino with Alzheimer's.* But Anne didn't seem dismayed in the slightest.

"Think hard, Glenda. Concentrate. Tell us exactly what happened and we'll get you fixed up with something to drink afterward, okay? What did these people who burned the poor dog want?"

"Well, shit, the first time, they wanted Charlie."

"The first time?"

"They was here twice," she said, nodding. "The first time was in the daylight, and they was looking for Charlie, only he wasn't around. Then they came back after dark and wanted Charlie's box, is what they said. Lots of people was looking for that thing, all freaking day and night. They said they found his squat, but his box wasn't there. That didn't make no sense to me. I mean, his squat *was* his box, wasn't it? Anyway, first there was Elmer Fudd with his weird hat and then and then these guys with the guns and the gas cans and finally these two Bobsey Twins in black suits. The twins told them they better go. They was mad."

"And did you know where this box was?"

"I didn't, but I think some of the guys mighta. I don't think Charlie even lived here. He hung around here a lot, but when night'd come, he'd go someplace else. We didn't tell nobody nothin', though. We wouldn't. People don't understand that.

After you lived on the streets for long enough, you can't be threatened anymore, is the thing. What do people got, to scare you with? Pain? Cold? Hell, they's old friends. Death? Who gives a shit? A broken arm or leg? That's a trip to a nice warm hospital with good food. I got to admit, the fire was pretty scary, and they had some really big guns, but killing the dog mostly just pissed us off. I mean, he wasn't a *great* dog or anything, but he didn't hurt nobody."

"So who were the guys with the guns?" I asked again. "More agents? Cops?"

"Don't put words in her mouth," said Anne, half under her breath.

"No, man, they was soldiers."

"You mean like uniform security guards?"

"You gonna tell me what I mean now? When I say soldiers, I mean soldiers. They didn't have their regular uniforms on or nothin, but you could tell. The way they talked, the way they moved. Even the way they had their hair cut. And they all had those funny looking boots they wear nowadays, the kind they don't have to polish?"

"Herman, why don't you go and get us some coffee and something to eat."

"Sausage biscuits," said Glenda the Witch. "I like them."

"Sausage biscuits," said Anne.

"And some red."

"And a bottle of wine," said Anne. "Glenda here has a lot of things to tell me, don't you dear?"

"I'll curl your fucking hair, is what."

"There's a sweetheart. Run along, Herman."

〈〉〈〉〈〉

Forty-five minutes later I was back, with the finest gourmet sandwiches that the SuperAmerica in Lowertown had plus a bottle of red wine so cheap, I wondered if it was safe to drink. I picked it mainly because it had a screw top. I figured if I had gotten one that needed a corkscrew, Glenda the Witch might just have opened it with a brick and wound up drinking the broken glass. Somebody once told me that was the homeless person's equivalent of having it on the rocks. The guy who told me that thought it was a joke.

When I got back, Anne Packard was sitting on a large rock, letting Glenda talk into a hand-held tape recorder, nodding encouragement now and then. They stopped when they saw me.

"Did you get the good stuff?" said Glenda.

"Did you earn it?"

"She did, Herman. Go ahead and give it to her."

Glenda opened the bottle first and had a big slug. She paused and looked off into space for a moment, as if she was pondering some great truth, and then she had another, bigger than the first. Then she screwed the top back on and made the bottle disappear somewhere inside her layers of clothes. Finally, she dug greedily into the paper bag with the sandwiches.

"How many ketchup you get? Looks like two."

"That would be because two is what it is."

"Didn't your mama teach you nothin? Something's free, you take all of it you can get." Her face darkened and she rummaged harder. "Ketchup, mustard, salt, napkins. Them are staples, man!" Her voice was rapidly escalating to hysteria-pitch.

"I'll remember, Glenda." To Anne, in a much lower tone, I said, "Time to leave."

"We're not quite done."

"I'm afraid we are." I gently took an elbow and tried to steer her away. Meanwhile, Glenda was working herself up to full frenzy.

"Next time? What the hell good's that do me, that 'next time' shit? You go back and get the rest of that stuff now, or I'll kick your ass, is what I'll do." She was screaming now. "Who the hell you think you are anyway? You come down here with your fancy clothes and your camera and shit, and you think you can cheat me. You think I'm nobody but…"

We walked away and left her ranting. When we got back up on high ground, Anne said, "What on earth was that all about?"

"Apparently Glenda is a mean drunk. Also a bipolar one, with maybe a touch of schizophrenia or alcoholic dementia here and there."

"But she only had the two drinks."

"You don't have a lot of experience with winos, do you? After enough years of pickling their brains in the sauce, the well-known trend of 'increased tolerance' starts to go the other way. They might go through a quart a day for years, and then one day they find they can get higher than a kite just by licking the cork."

"That's terrible."

"Well, yes. Life on the street is terrible. Maybe that's what you ought to be writing about. Not that it's exactly a new topic."

"So are you telling me that all the stuff I just got from her is just drunken delusions?"

"No, I'm not. She's probably never really sober, but she was at least dry when you were taping her. Did she say she was dry when the soldiers came to the gulch?"

"I think so. She had a lot of stuff to say, most of it totally beside the point, but I think she said that, yes."

"Then you should be all right. The cops would write her off because they couldn't count on her in court, but you don't have that problem."

"No, I only have the problem of getting two corroborating sources. Sometimes I think it might be easier to be a cop."

"Do reporters actually do that, that two-source business?"

"I do."

Back downtown, we went up into the skyway system at its eastern end, through the lobby of the former Buckby-Meers Building, where I'm told there used to be a real Foucault pendulum. I've never figured out what purpose it served, taking the pendulum out. A block or two farther on, I pointed to another deli and gave Anne an enquiring look. She pointed to her watch and shook her head, no, and we headed back toward her office.

"So what do you think?" I said. "Do you have a story?"

"Oh, it's a story, all right. But I can't see what it's about yet. It's at the stage we call holding a monster by the tail. I still need the hook, something to hang it all on. Until I get that, I really can't write it."

"That makes sense. I don't know what it's all about, either, but I intend to find out."

"Well, when you do, give me a call. Here's my card, with my direct line. I'll write my cell phone number on it, too." She proceeded to scribble as we walked, looking up from time to time.

"And here's my office," she said. "So I'll say goodbye now. Pam, would you please give this gentleman back his box?"

"Some people from his office came and picked it up, Miss Packard. They said he needed it right away." She smiled sweetly, as if she were expecting a pat on the head.

"What did they look like?" I said.

"Well, like you two, sort of. Business people. Not crooks or anything."

"A man and a woman?" I said. "Dark, severe clothes, very formal, superior manner?"

"Yes, that sounds right. So they were your people, then?"

"No, they were not. I think they were spooks, actually, but I would definitely like to see the tapes from your surveillance cameras for that time slot."

"I don't know if we can do that."

"Herman," said Anne, suddenly very serious, "that wasn't it, was it?"

"What wasn't what?"

"Don't be cute. Was that Charles Victor's box, the one everybody is supposed to be looking for?"

"No, it was a decoy. And somebody just bit on it."

"But you know where the real one is?"

"Possibly."

"Now you're being cute again."

"Let's say I can lay my hands on *a box* that used to belong to Charlie. He thought it was important for somebody to keep it for him. I have never looked inside it."

"Is that my hook?"

"I won't know until I look inside it, will I?"

"Fair enough."

"You can go with me to get it, if you want. First, though, I think we should go visit your friend at the County Morgue."

"Why on earth?"

"I'm Charlie's sole heir. I can claim his personal effects, whatever they might be. And I should do so before they all get shipped off to some lab that won't tell us what they find."

"Pam? Sign me out for the rest of the day."

Fire in the City

Anne's contact person down at the Morgue turned out to be a young lab technician named Brian Faraday. It was obvious that it made him very nervous, having us back in the restricted spaces. It was also obvious that he was totally infatuated with Anne and would do almost anything to keep from displeasing her.

Looking at Charlie's body didn't tell us much, apart from the fact that both life and death had been very cruel to him. His meager collection of personal possessions wasn't just a fountainhead of information, either. Brian wouldn't let me have any, but he let us have a look at them, in a zippered plastic bag that was on its way to the evidence room in the main cop shop. So apparently they were calling it a homicide, after all.

There wasn't much there. There were his original army dog tags, of course. Why he had kept them all this time, I couldn't imagine, but I knew the police had used them to ID him more than once before, since he had held neither a driver's license nor a Social Security card. There was a small comb with a few teeth missing, a pocketknife, a combination can opener and corkscrew, a few coins, a dirty bandanna. Half a candy bar. And an ace of spades from a deck with the horse-head insignia on the back. The death card he had told his lawyer about.

"Air Cav," I said, pointing to it.

"Are you an expert on military insignias?"

"Not even slightly. But that was Charlie's old outfit. He had a shoulder patch on his fatigue jacket, just like it."

The bag also contained some kind of key, a stubby little brass thing, very thick and solid.

"I don't suppose we could get something to drink," I said to our host. "Coffee or a soda, maybe?" Anne gave me a perplexed look and I nodded my head ever so slightly, trying to cue her to go along with me.

"Um, you're not going to hang around here or anything, are you?" said young Brian, even more nervous than before.

"No, no. I, ah, just got a little queasy, looking at poor old Charlie back there. I could really use a little drink of something to settle my stomach."

"Maybe a can of pop?" said Anne. "Thanks so very much, Brian."

And the moonstruck lad was off in a flash. As soon as he was out of sight, I dug a stick of gum out of my pocket, peeled the wrapper off it, and made two quick imprints, one each of the end and side of the key. Gum was hardly the preferred medium for a pattern, but it was what I had. Then I held the key out to Anne with the face that had a serial number on it toward her.

"Shoot," I said. "Close-up, if you can."

"I can."

She shot three quick pictures of the key and we immediately stuck it back in the plastic bag. Then I put the stick of gum back in its wrapper and slipped it into my shirt pocket, where it wouldn't be too likely to get bent out of shape. As I was tucking it away, the lab techie came back, bearing a hopeful smile and a can of iced tea.

"Jesus," I said under my breath. "Why did he pick tea? I really hate tea."

"Not today, you don't," said Anne, out of the corner of her mouth. Out loud, she said, "Oh, that's so thoughtful, Brian. Thank you again."

While he beamed at her, I put a tiny bit of the nasty brew in my mouth and a bunch of it down the drain of a service sink. My memory was dead-on correct, for a change; I really do hate tea. I pretended to drink a bit more and then asked Brian the thing that had been eating at me.

"What happens to the body?"

"We keep it for a while, until we know for sure if the detectives want any other tests done. After that, if nobody comes to claim it, we cremate it."

"You burn it." I didn't like that idea at all.

"Well, that would be how you cremate somebody, yeah."

"Yeah but I mean..." I drew in a deep breath.

"It's not like he's going to feel it, or anything."

"Don't we have something like Potters' Field in Minnesota? I mean—"

"Cremation," he said, folding his arms and shaking his head. "We do it right over there."

He pointed at something that looked like an antique furnace, bulky, rusty, and machine ugly. In fact, it looked a lot like the furnace from my old pad in Detroit.

And suddenly, there it was. With a gasp and a chill, I had tripped back to a time and place I was sure I had left forever, never wanted to think about again. I was back in Detroit in the blistering summer of 1967. I was fourteen years old, and in a broken-bottle landscape backlit by burning buildings, I was running for my life.

<>‹›<>

You hear the term "Rust Belt" a lot these days, but I don't believe in it. A lot of the old factories along the Detroit River have moved out or just shut down, but Henry Ford's River Rouge plant and GM's Cadillac factory farther to the north are still cranking out shiny chrome-trimmed monsters, the railroads are still busy feeding the iron giant and hauling away its products, and the diners and bars and dance halls are full every night. Everybody works and plays. Everybody is singing Motown, and everybody is buying tickets to tomorrow. Life is good.

Pretty good, anyway. The folks who have good jobs work hard and get by. Those who can't break into the unions or the decent housing, which mostly means blacks, don't. They tend to be some of Uncle Fred's best customers, since their chances in the normal world are rotten to none. Sometimes that translates into despair but just as often it morphs seamlessly into rage. And sometimes the two are hard to tell apart. When the heat goes up in the center city, there seems to be plenty of both.

There are neighborhoods where a white boy like me has no business wandering around on his own. And there are others where no kid of any color wants to let the sun go down and find him still on the street. That's too bad, since a lot of my Uncle Fred's customers are in those neighborhoods, and sometimes it's my turn to help with the collections.

Besides the normal bookie business of taking bets on horse races and sports contests of all kinds, my uncle also sells tickets to the New York lottery, since Michigan doesn't have one of its own. He lets me take the orders on the phone. I copy down the requested number and read it back to the caller, along with their name and address. When I've sold twenty or so, I call one of half a dozen numbers for our layoff men in New York itself, and he calls me back a little later to confirm that he's bought the actual tickets. We charge our customers five dollars for a fifty-cent ticket, don't mess with the quarter or dollar tickets at all. In the unlikely event that the customer's number actually hits, we split the winnings right down the middle. I've only seen that happen once, and I was dumbfounded to hear an out-of-work upholsterer's helper bitching about only getting thirty-five thousand dollars.

On a good day, when nobody wastes my time with a lot of chitchat, I can sell a hundred and twenty tickets, make a record of who I sold them to, and get the actual tickets bought, some thousand or so miles away. My pay for all that is ten percent of the markup, or forty-five cents a ticket, which translates to fifty-four dollars a day.

That is just purely one hell of a lot of money for a teenage kid, more than enough for me to have my own place, upstairs over a rundown hardware store on the near West Side. Fred calls it "a two-room flop, upstairs over a used paint store," but it's a big deal for me. I don't intend ever to go back to high school or to my mother's house up on Seven Mile, with its floating array of boyfriends whom I refuse to call stepfathers. I intend to be a mojo numbers man, just like my uncle.

We have several freelance contractors working at collecting the five bucks a pop from all those customers, and I don't know what their cut is, except that it's more than mine. But that's okay, because their job is tougher.

Once or twice a week, Uncle Fred tells me to tag along with one or another of them, just to see all the facets of the business close up, practice for the day when I'm big enough to pinch-hit at any position. For those trips, I don't get paid anything. It's just on-the-job training. I carry a sturdy leather gym bag to put the money in and a baseball bat to protect it with. Uncle Fred doesn't let me carry a gun.

I usually go with a big Irishman about twice my age, named Gerry Phearson, or Jerp for short. He's ten feet tall and has baseball mitts for hands and bulldozers for feet, and everybody says he looks like John Wayne with stringy red hair. They also say that if you get him mad enough, he can kick a hole in a cinder-block wall or bite the numbers off a billiard ball.

He likes me. When people say, "Hey Jerp, who's riding shotgun for you today?" he will tell them, "Me little brother, boyo, and don't you be giving him no grief, or I'll let him break your kneecaps for you." We drive around in a beat-up '59 Mercury and park any damn where we like.

The heat wave this July is brutal, and we have all the windows down and wet rags on our heads. Swamp Arabs, Jerp calls us. I think we look so totally stupid, we're cool. We're overdue to collect on about a hundred bucks worth of tickets up in Highland Park, where the first big Ford plant was once, and over on the near West Side. There were some riots over there a couple nights ago, and we stayed away from the area to let it cool down. On Twelfth Street, right in the heart of the neighborhood, the cops made an early morning raid on a blind pig, and a hundred or so drunk customers decided they would rather attack the cops than stand around waiting for a fleet of paddy wagons to show up and take them off in chains. To hear the news reports, it turned into a major war.

But we've had blowups before, between angry blacks and angrier white cops. The situation ought to be cool enough to touch by now.

Rounding the corner off Grand Boulevard onto Dexter, I can see that cool is exactly what it is not. A huge crowd of blacks, mostly young men, is swarming over the street, while behind them, buildings are going up in flames, one after another. We might have another ten minutes before the whole sky is covered with dirty brown-black clouds and the cinders come raining down everywhere. Off to the east, I can see the flashing lights of some fire trucks, but it's obvious they're never going to get through the mob.

There's gunfire now, too. I can't tell if any of it is aimed at us, but there's a lot of it.

"Jerp, I hate to be the one to say it, but maybe we should get the hell out of here."

"We've still got collections to make, lad. It sets a bad precedent, letting a fish off the hook over a little thing like a riot."

"What about the guns?"

"Which ones?"

Which ones? Is he crazy? "The ones that seem to be going off all around us just now."

"Ah, those. Sort of like Sunday in Belfast, isn't it? Makes a body homesick, it does. Now, if one of our customers had a gun, that might be different. I'd have to make him eat it, wouldn't I? But these guns have nothing to do with us at all, at all. The jungle people are shooting up their own, most likely. Or they're shooting the cops, which of course would be a terrible shame."

I can see there's no point talking to him. He's got himself set on showing me how unflappable he is, I guess, and once he makes up his mind, you might as well argue with a statue. Typical Irish, my Uncle Fred would say. Rock solid from the ground up, right through the brain.

I wish I felt as cool as he acts. I've got a prickly little animal running around in my gut that says the day is going to get very ugly before it's finally over.

The crowd gets closer and larger, and Jerp steers the big Merc' over the curb and through a trash-strewn parking lot as some rocks and bricks start to hit the car and a lot of guys are swinging big sticks and surging toward us. Behind us, a Molotov cocktail goes up with a dull "whoof," maybe meant for us, maybe not.

Jerp is picking up speed now, despite people swarming in on all sides. Wire grocery carts and trash cans go flying off the front bumper and into the crowd, as he tries to get enough momentum up to crash through the cyclone fence at the back of the lot.

A metallic screech, a lot of jolts and tearing noises, and we're through, heading down a wide industrial alley. All around us, black men are grabbing sticks or metal bars, pounding on the car as we plow through them. Occasionally we bounce a sweaty black body off the grille.

"Lock your door, lad."

He doesn't have to tell me twice.

More gunfire. Loud, hoarse barks that I recognize as shotgun blasts, and other higher-pitched popping that must be pistol fire. A few bodies down on the pavement now, some of them in spreading pools of blood. We sure as hell didn't shoot them. I wonder who did.

If all that weren't enough, now we have machine gun fire. Tracer rounds are stitching a line across the second story fire escapes of a clapboard tenement down the street. The neon line of bullets comes first, the brrt-brrt noise a second or two later, sounding muffled. The shooter is a long way away, maybe as much as a mile. He's shooting at something else altogether, something we will never see, or at nothing at all. But what goes up must come down, and unfortunately, it's still lethal.

"Herman, lad, do you know how to drive?"

"Yeah, sure." The car has an automatic transmission. How hard could it be? I look over at him and I see blood coming out of his mouth and the big, meaty hands white on the steering wheel.

"Jesus, Jerp—"

"Just grab the wheel, will you? You don't have to worry about the brake, because we're not stopping. Head for downtown. The old Michigan Central train depot. The place has been next thing to abandoned for years. We ought to be able to find a place inside there to lay low for a while and maybe stash the money. Or if we can't, we'll take a train out. If we try to get back to the office with the dough and run into the cops or the National Guard, they'll relieve us of it, and that's a certainty."

He lets go of the wheel and floors the gas pedal, and I suddenly find out that steering really isn't very tough at all, if you don't care what you hit.

We're back on Grand, heading east and south, the big engine pushing us up toward seventy. I blow the horn at anything that gets in our way, bounce off a few busses and cars, and mostly aim right down the center of the street, ignoring all the traffic lights. Jerp is breathing in gasps now and clutching a red handkerchief to his side, but he's still conscious and his eyes look clear.

Two blocks ahead, I see a wall of khaki. The National Guard or the Army, hundreds of them or maybe thousands, with trucks and jeeps, are blocking off the street, advancing en masse.

"Ease off, Jerp. I think we're okay now."

"With that lot? Bollocks. First we have to stash the money."

"It's only money, Jerp. There will always be money. We have to get you—"

"It's the responsibility, is the thing. We lose somebody else's money, we're no better than that riffraff we just left. Find a place to stash it, I say!" He's screaming through clenched teeth now, and again I see there's no point in arguing.

"We're not too far from my place," I say. "I've got a secret stash in the basement of the hardware store that we—"

"Go for it, lad!"

I make the corner onto Hobson on two wheels, and Jerp eases off on the gas a bit and lets me maneuver into the side streets.

"Almost there," I say. "How are you holding up?"

"Alls I need is a short beer and a shot of Bushnell's, and I'd be singing 'Molly Malone.' Shut up and drive."

Three more turns and we're there. Jerp can't seem to find the brake pedal, so I throw the shifting lever into Park. The transmission makes a noise like a mechanical pig being slaughtered, but finally the rear wheels lock up and we skid to a stop in the alley behind the hardware store.

"Quick now, lad."

As if he had to tell me. The streets are deserted here, but I can hear shouting mobs not that far off. I grab the gym bag, pile out of the car, and use my key to let myself into the service entry of the store. Lights off, everything deserted. I wonder where Mr. Holst, the owner, would go, if he decided to evacuate his own neighborhood. Where would anybody go?

Down in the basement, I open up the fire door on the old monster coal furnace that has long ago been replaced by the new gas-fired Lennox. I stick my body half inside the fire chamber, pick up the edge of the sheet of asbestos board that covers my own personal money stash, and throw the gym bag under it. As I shut the door and sprint for the stairs, I hear gunfire out in the alley.

Oh, shit. We cut it too fine.

Maybe I should have brought Jerp inside with me. Maybe I still should. Go ask. But my feet aren't moving. It feels safe in the basement. And I am so very afraid. I dither and hesitate and wait, for what, I don't know. And then I see the smoke at the top of the stairs. The bastards have torched my building.

Stairs three at a time, kick the back door open again, don't bother with turning out the lights. The deadbolt will relock itself, if there's anything left to protect. Just be sure you've still got your key.

Back outside, the sunlight is blinding. I put my hand up to shield my eyes, just in time to catch a blow from a club. Jesus, it feels like my forearm is shattered. With my other hand, I swing the baseball bat, lashing out blindly in all directions. I catch at least one set of shins and maybe a head or two, and I'm able to clear a little free space around myself.

Everything looks black and white but slowed down now, like an old movie being run in slow motion. I must have a lot of sweat in my eyes, because it's getting hard to focus.

Down the street, somebody yells, "Hey man, they broke open Ullman's!" That would be the neighborhood liquor store. The mob surges that way and loses interest in me. I make a final clearing swing or two with the bat and head back to where I left Jerp and the car.

Neither of which is there anymore.

What the hell?

He was hurt too bad to drive off himself, but if somebody was just boosting the car, wouldn't they have dumped him out first? I climb the steel fire escape from my own pad, to get a better look over the crowd, but even so, car and Irishman are absolutely, totally gone. And as I perch there, they are joined by my pad, my building, my stash. And all my dreams. The building is going up so fast, the flames are already scorching my back.

I bound back to ground level and fight my way through the fringes of the crowd to some fairly clear street to the south. Then I start to make my way back toward downtown, running from one hiding place to another. The old Michigan Central train depot, Jerp had said. If he was capable of moving under his own power at all, that's where he would go, and that's where I should go, too.

Get there before dark, though, boyo. If you don't, you're just as likely to be killed by somebody inside the building as out.

How long is it until dark, anyway? The day is already about thirty hours old and looking like a place with no end.

Is that as fast as you can run, Herman? Cry, if you have to, maybe also scream. Piss your pants, if you think that helps anything. But whatever you do, do not stop running. Because once that goddamn sun goes down, the only white folks left on these streets are going to be the very quick and the very dead.

Jerp, where the hell are you?

‹›‹›‹›

"Herman?"

I blinked.

"Are you all right, Herman?"

"Sure." Not even slightly.

"Do you want to claim this body?" said Brian.

"I'm not sure what I want yet." I gave him one of my cards. "Don't burn him without calling me first, okay?"

Dead Man's Key

We thanked Brian for all his help and went back out on the street.

"Well, that certainly didn't gain us much," said Anne.

"Maybe, maybe not. How quick can you get me a print of that key photo?"

"If we go back to my office, I can run one in two minutes, flat. What are you going to do with it?"

"Take it to a pawnbroker friend of mine who also happens to be a locksmith, see what he makes of it."

"And also have him make you an illegal copy?"

"Are you so sure it would be illegal? I mean, I really am Charlie's heir, you know."

"I think I don't want to hear about it."

"You're probably right, you don't want to."

⟨⟩⟨⟩⟨⟩

We walked back to the skyway reception area again, and I did a poor job of making small talk with Pam while Anne took her camera to some inner sanctum to do her thing with it. As good as her word, she was back in less than five minutes with an eight-and-a-half by eleven color print.

"It's a little grainy at this enlargement size," she said, "but the serial number comes up all right."

"That should do very nicely. If it's a real key, from a real lock company, my guy should be able to look it up."

"The bad news is, we shouldn't have come back here."

"Oh?"

"I ran into my editor, who was tactless enough to remind me that I have a deadline for a column I haven't started yet. I'm going to have to pass on going to see your locksmith."

"Tell you what: you go do your column and I'll go do the things you don't want to know about. And later this evening, I'll take a look inside Charlie's box and call you on your cell if I find anything that looks important."

"Call me no matter what you find. I won't shut the phone off until I've heard from you."

"Deal."

"Later."

"Happy column." I thought about inviting her to a romantic candlelit dinner of takeout Chinese with a cigar box instead of a fortune cookie. I thought about it rather a lot, in fact. But if she was sending me any of the right signals for such a venture, I couldn't read them. I sighed slightly and headed back down the skyway.

Nickel Pete's was only a couple of blocks away, but instead of going straight there, I took the skyway system all the way to the City Hall Annex. Whether my friendly shadows had found my phony cigar box amusing or not, I figured they would still be following me.

At the Annex, I took the elevator to the basement, then picked a lock to let myself into a stairwell to the sub-basement. Some remnants of my old life skills are handy at times. I re-locked the door behind me and went down to the original boiler room, now covered in dust and cobwebs, where I waited. Five minutes later, somebody rattled the knob from the other side. Then he kicked the door twice. Then nothing.

I waited another ten minutes, then headed back north through a maze of forgotten storage spaces and mechanical rooms. All of the sub-basements on that block are connected, and I finally came back out into the daylight through a freight elevator at the far end of the block, where I turned up my collar, put my head down, and sprinted the block and a half to Nickel Pete's pawn shop.

He was about as happy to see me as he had been the last time.

"It's too late for lunch now, Herman, so what kind of weird favor are you going to hit me up for this time?"

"Good to see you, too, Pete. Always a pleasure. I have a picture to show you."

"Is it pornographic? Will it awaken long-forgotten urges and incite unwise adventures?"

"Afraid not." I unfolded the print and laid it out on his counter, along with the impressed stick of gum, which really hadn't fared all that well in my pocket.

"Then what's the point?"

"Just look at it, will you?"

He looked.

"Do you have a book of some kind where you can look up the serial number of that key?" I asked.

"What for?"

"Is this what they call a senior moment? To tell what it is, of course."

"I don't have to look it up, I know what it is. It's a Master."

"That's probably why it says 'Master' on it. I picked up on that already. Can you look up the serial number and tell me what it fits?"

"Obviously Herman, you were having a little nap when I said the word 'Master.' Master only makes padlocks."

"So?"

"Millions and gazillions of padlocks. The most you might find out is the name of some hardware wholesaler, who is most likely out of business for ages now."

"Why do you say that?"

"Because the number is only four digits. That baby is *old*, Herman."

"Well, bat shit, Pete."

"Now I expect you're going to ask me if I can make you a copy, using nothing but the photo and that mangled piece of chewing gum for a pattern."

"Pete, you really should have made a career on the stage. You can read minds perfectly."

"How nice for me. But instead, I'm stuck here, breaking the law and putting my locksmith's license in jeopardy." He let out a profound sigh and headed for the back room. "The things I do for you."

It was favorite line of his.

While Pete made the key, I watched the storefront and main door, looking for shadows on the other side of the glass that I might want to hide from. Then I grabbed the phone from Pete's side of the counter and called Wilkie's cell phone.

"Harra." He always answers that way, and I have never figured out what it means.

"Hey, Wide, Herman here. How's your work load?"

"Your man Russo hasn't left town yet. Unless he tries to leave the country, I can't grab him before his trial date, so I got one of my second-stringers keeping an eye on him."

"That'll work. So are you available for something else?"

"Well, seeing as how I failed to pick up any loose change last night when my eight-ball shooter split on me, I could use a little something, you know? Not for tonight, though. I got a date."

"Would that be with the ugly broad from the Minneapolis cop shop?"

"Hey, watch your mouth. She's a nice person."

"Me? You're the one who always calls her that. I've never even met her. Anyway, is that the lucky lady?"

"So?"

"I'm wondering if you can hit her up for a favor."

"The number of dates she gets? I can hit her up."

"Now who's saying mean things about her?"

"Well it's not like she's listening, is it? What are you after?"

"Go by my office and pick up a snow shovel that's wrapped in a black plastic trash bag. Don't open it unless you've got gloves on. I need somebody who knows what they're doing to see if they can pull some fingerprints off it."

"And then see if those prints are on record."

"Well it would be a pretty pointless exercise otherwise, wouldn't it?"

"What do I use for an excuse?"

"You'll think of something."

"But this is a bounty hunting job, right?"

"We'll call it that, anyway." Wilkie doesn't have a PI license, and sometimes we have to do a little creative labeling of the work he does for me. Bounty hunting doesn't require a license.

"Who am I hunting besides Russo?"

"Whoever's prints are on the shovel."

"Uh huh. And who am I hunting before I know who that is?"

"Joe Kapufnik. The Duke of Paducah. I don't care. Have Agnes pull a couple of names out of our 'long-gone' file. And tell her I said to give you a couple hundred retainer out of petty cash. Take your friend someplace nice."

"Hey, you're right. I'll think of something. Anything else?"

"One other thing. This one's a little more open-ended and not so quick. See what you can find out about a guy who calls himself Eddie Bardot, claims to work for something called Amalgamated Bonding Enterprises. He was in my office this morning, so my security tape will still have him on it. Aggie can print you a still photo off it, if you see a frame you like. Either his name or the company's could be phony, but he doesn't look as if he ever changed his face. Give it a shot, okay?"

"What are you liking him for?"

"I'm not sure. He comes off like old Mob, but he could be just a freelance shakedown artist trying to look that way. Before I decide how to deal with him, I need to know if he's connected."

"Time and expenses-plus-ten?"

"That's the drill, only I might not be able to pay you right away."

"I can wait. I'm on it."

"What's your girl's name?"

"None of your business."

"Odd name. Say hi for me."

Pete brought me the key, and I left.

Charlie Victor's Box

I left Pete's by the back way, through an L-shaped alley, and went straight to the Victory Ramp, where I retrieved my BMW, after carefully looking over the undercarriage and the wheel wells to see if it had acquired any bugs or bombs. If it had, they were extremely tiny, so I decided they couldn't hurt me.

If my tail included one or more vehicles, I couldn't spot them. But just to be on the safe side, I took a very indirect route home. I crossed the Mrs. Hippy on the Robert Street Bridge and wandered around the river flats for a while, then headed up the Wabasha hill to the top of the river bluffs, to an area known as Cherokee Heights. There I got on the high end of the long, straight, severely sloping High Bridge and went back down across the river again. But at the bottom of the bridge, I made a strictly illegal U-turn and headed back up. As I went back the way I had come, I did a mental inventory of the oncoming traffic.

White Taurus with Parks and Rec markings, blue Corolla with about a dozen little kids in the back seat, dark green Mini Cooper with a lone woman in it, kind of cute, red Chevy pickup with dopey-looking decals and a couple of young guys with backward baseball caps, dirty black Hummer, some kind of small Pontiac in metallic brown. All of them had Minnesota plates, except for the Hummer, which had no license on the front.

At the top of the bridge, I turned right onto a narrow parkway, went around a couple of blocks, and finally turned back south onto Smith Avenue, heading across the bridge yet again. And again, I looked at the oncoming traffic.

Dodge Intrepid, Honda Civic, big box Chevy, PT Cruiser, Hummer.

A dirty black Hummer with no front plate. Very careless, guys.

Unfortunately, the glass on the monster was too dirty or too heavily tinted for me to see who was in it.

The speed limit on the High Bridge is forty. But if I were going to pick up a cop, my goofy U-turn would have already done the job. So I took the rest of the bridge at seventy. At the bottom of it, I ran the gear box on the 328i down into second and made a hard left, accelerating through the turn in a nice, four-wheel power drift, just on the verge of out of control. Forty going in, sixty coming out, and gone in a blink. Any Hummer trying that would be found upside down, a quarter of a mile down Smith Avenue. I blew into the tangled web of narrow streets to the north and west, made a few more turns, and finally parked the car in the customer lot of a body shop. Then I locked it and walked back south through the alleys, to my condo. I didn't see the Hummer again.

My condo is a two-story stone-clad row house, in the middle of an attached cluster of six others just like it. They are a hundred and twenty years old, restored and gone to seed again more times than anybody can remember anymore. If the stone on the outside were dirtier and rough, instead of newly sandblasted and smooth, and if the whole building were located a couple thousand miles farther east, you would call it a brownstone. It has high ceilings, multi-paned windows, and walls that you couldn't punch through with a bazooka. And it's on a short side street that gets no through traffic at all. I like it.

I checked both front and back doors, to see if they had been worked on. They have electronic lock monitors that Pete rigged up for me. If either of them had been opened while I was gone, all the monitors would be flashing tiny red lights at me. Inside, a light on my phone would also be flashing, but no message would go out to the police or anybody else. Satisfied that everything was as I had left it, I went back outside to an old-fashioned sloped cellar door on the end of the entire building complex and worked the combination on the padlock.

The townhouses have the unusual feature of having a single, undivided common basement. Since that has been a violation of about sixteen kinds of building and fire codes for a century or so, the last set of renovators solved the problem by giving no unit any direct access to the space. Instead, the basement has an unbroken fireproof ceiling with no stairs going up into anybody's house, including mine. My furnace and water heater are in a closet off the kitchen.

Silly as it sounds, that makes the basement a good place to hide things, if only because most search warrants will not be written to cover a space that isn't exactly in the same building. At least, I thought so. The general clutter of cardboard boxes and broken appliances and antiques with no names would make searching a real undertaking, too. But the real goodie was the dirt floor. I had done nothing any more clever with Charlie's box than put it in a plastic bag and bury it. I buried it right in front of the basement's only door, where I figured the dirt would get packed back down quickly by whatever traffic there might be. Then I left a small shovel for myself inside an old laundry tub, as far from the door as it could possibly be.

I don't know if any of that was really clever or not, but it worked. The box was still there.

It seemed awfully large for a cigar box, but it clearly had a label that said Rigoletto Palma Cedars, so I didn't think it was a tackle box. It was well made, out of solid wood, with brass hardware, and it had a stamped-on trademark of some importer on it. I threw the plastic bag in the trashcan by the back alley and took the box inside. I put it on the kitchen counter while I reset my lock system. Then I checked for any obvious booby traps or notes warning of booby traps on the box. Finally, I flipped up the brass hasp and opened it.

It was full of junk. War medals, old coins, expired coupons, free passes to places that didn't exist anymore. Bus tokens for lines that had made their last stops ages ago. Also lists of names and phone numbers, and mailing addresses torn from yellowed envelopes. Little people's treasures, the kind of crap that the kids closing out their parents' estates never know what to do with.

And at the very bottom of the box, there was a ledger. An old-fashioned green-page ledger and a loose-leaf scrapbook, showing what people gave him and what they wanted in return, with inserted notes in dozens of different writing hands.

At first I thought they were all the stuff of pure fantasy, vouchers to be drawn on the First National Bank of Neverland. But the more of them I read, the less I thought so. Charlie had often said that for all his other faults, not the least of which was being a self-proclaimed murderer, he was always a man of his word. His markers were good, he said, and I believed him. But these were some damned strange markers.

A typical note in the scrapbook read, "Here's these two ten dollar bills I been saved since my graduation party at the rehab center, twelve year ago. I never touch them till now. Bet them along with what you want of your own on Bottom Jewel in the Exacta, and if he wins, put everything in the pot for B."

There was a date on the note, and when I looked up the same date in the ledger, I found the following entry:

Bottom Jewel 40:1 to win, 25:1 to place. $800 to pot, 6/29/97. Tally now $17,250. Hook says he wants an even 20k. Balance to big box.

It wasn't possible. I mean, Bottom Jewel was possible, but no way Charlie accumulated thirty grand, or even seventeen, by always betting on the right horse. Where the hell did he get the rest of his money? I took the papers to my dining room table, where I could spread them out a bit. Then I laid out a fresh pack of cigarettes and a clean ashtray from the living room and a bottle of Scotch and a tumbler from the hall closet, and sat down to go to work.

I looked for entries in the ledger that had dollar amounts but no references to any bets, and then I looked for notes with the same dates. The first one I found blew me away.

> Wells Fargo Downtown. Six guards, all armed. Two of them know how to handle themselves. Security cameras too high to spray or disable. Vault closed. $200 to big box.

There was a similar note for the Bremmer Bank, which was also downtown, and several for grocery or liquor stores, which were not.

I was stunned. Burnout case or not, Charlie was apparently coherent and focused enough to be a point man for a bunch of professional robbers. It would have been easy enough for him. Bumble into the lobby, practice a little aggressive panhandling, and get himself thrown out by the security staff. He could pick up a lot of information that way, and after they threw him out, people were unlikely to bother to have him arrested.

So it was possible that Charlie had a large stash, at that. Then the question became what he did with it.

Partway through the second Scotch, I found a list of names. No notes, just names. Some had check marks in front of them. They were not famous names like the President or some senator or T. Boone Pickens, but I knew a few of them. One was a judge, one a parole officer, and one a cop. They all had checks by their names and if memory served, all of them were dead.

It suddenly occurred to me that in his own strange and twisted way, Charlie had been in the business of selling hope. It was a very angry and bitter variety, the hope of some hated authority figure getting offed. But it was hope, all the same, the stuff that made somebody's life just a little more bearable. Real or phony, he was in the business of letting little people believe they had a way to fight back at the establishment.

Of course, he had also been in the business of making the Secret Service and some kind of nameless military types extremely nervous. Nervous enough to kill him? I didn't know, but I intended to find out. I took another sip of Scotch, a very small one this time, and started to add up the numbers in the ledger.

One other thing mystified me: if everything I was seeing was what it seemed, why had Charlie let me hold the box for him? He had given it to me two years earlier and never asked to see it again. Curiouser and curiouser.

An hour later, I called Anne Packard from the wall phone out in my central hallway and told her I had found her hook. The doorbell rang in the middle of our call.

"Are you expecting company?" she said.

"No, and it's too late at night for the Jehovah's Witnesses or the cute little girls selling cookies. Hang on a minute, will you?"

"I'll be here."

I put down the phone as quietly as I could and quickly went back to the kitchen and took my .380 Beretta out of its plastic bag in the vegetable crisper of the refrigerator. As I passed the phone again, the little red light was flashing frantically.

A Deal With the Devil

My house has a storm entry, with about four feet between the inner and outer doors. I peeked through the edge of the leaded glass in the inner door and saw that my intruder was a familiar figure. I flattened myself against the adjacent wall and let her finish picking the inner lock. As she was opening the door, I threw a phone book down the hallway, and when she leaned forward to see what the noise was, I hooked my left arm around her neck, pulled her the rest of the way into the room, and pressed the Beretta against the base of her skull. She tried to put an elbow into my chest, but she had a poor angle, and it was easy to deflect. She also tried to stomp on my instep, but her aim was bad and all she managed to do was flatten my big toe a bit. She had a lean and athletic body, but she had definitely been neglecting her martial arts training.

"Good evening, Agent Krause. I'll take your sidearm now, please."

"You'll take your hands off me, is what you'll do. I have a no-knock warrant."

"I don't care if you have the goddamn Magna Carta. I'll take your weapon. Now. Spare us both the embarrassment of me pulling it out of some kind of holster between your thighs."

"You're putting yourself in a lot of trouble here, Mr. Jackson. For assaulting an agent, you can get thrown in a hole so deep and black, the best lawyer on earth will never find you."

"Is that what you told Charlie you were going to do to him? Is he dead because he believed you and let down his guard?"

"You don't really think that, do you? That's insane."

"So are black holes where lawyers can't find you. For all I know, so's the whole damn Department of Homeland Conspiracy. Now give up the piece." I pressed the barrel of the Beretta harder into her neck.

"All right," she said. "Just stay calm, okay? I'm going to move really slowly."

She started to reach down toward the hem of her skirt with her right hand, and I told her to stop and switch to her left. She did. And slowly, as she had promised, she produced some kind of very narrow, compact semi-automatic. Not standard Secret Service issue, I thought.

"Put it in my left hand," I said.

"Take your left hand off my neck."

"Actually, that's my forearm on your neck. But give me the gun, and we'll be all done with that, too."

She put the weapon in my hand, barrel first, and I told her to turn it around the right way. When she did, I held it out in front of us, reached down with my little finger, and tripped the lug to drop the magazine out. If she was impressed with that fantastically dexterous maneuver, she withheld her applause.

"Do you have a round in the chamber?"

"The place I carry that thing? Do you think I'm crazy?"

"No. Disagreeable, but definitely not crazy." But I flipped the safety off and pulled the trigger, all the same, pointing the gun at the floor. It really was empty. Then I let her step away from me and gestured to the living room and its big, overstuffed couch. When she sat down on it, I gave her back her gun.

"I'm going to show you the warrant now, okay?" She made a move toward her handbag, but I grabbed it away from her.

"No. Not okay."

"You need to see what you're violating, here."

"No, I don't. You need to see that I don't give a damn. If I shoot you, I'm not violating anything, I'm defending my home.

Any jury in the nation would say so. But if I decide you can be trusted, then maybe you don't need the warrant anyway."

"Oh, really? That's not how you were talking last time we met."

"I've been thinking since then that I might be open to some trading."

"We don't trade. We insist, and we get."

"We? I don't see your partner, Agent."

"He's probably inside the back door by now, about to come in here and blow you away." But she wasn't looking toward the back of the house. Instead, her eyes were turned down and to her right.

"No, he isn't. And from the look on your face, I don't believe he's coming, either."

There was also the small matter of the silent alarm. If her partner really were at the back door, I would be seeing two flashing red lights on the hallway phone, instead of just one. But I saw no reason to tell her that.

"Do you seriously think I would come here without my partner?"

And suddenly I saw it. And it was hilarious.

"You dumped him, didn't you?" I said. "I could see back in my office that you don't like the little twerp. But you don't trust him either, do you? That's why you came here alone. You probably didn't even tell him what you were up to."

"Goddamned arrogant little prick." She folded her arms tightly and found something to study in the pattern of my carpet.

"Him, or me?"

"I mean, stupidity is one thing, but aggressive, gleeful, pompous stupidity is inexcusable."

I guessed she meant him. I was starting to like this conversation a lot.

"Does he hit on you, too?"

She unfolded her arms and slapped the couch on either side.

"God! What is it with you guys? I mean, is that a given? No, he doesn't hit on me. That has too much finesse for him. He tried to rape me, is what he did."

"Oh, shit." Suddenly it had stopped being funny. "I'm sorry for you."

"You think *you're* sorry? Talk to him. I gave him a case of smashed balls that left him walking funny for a month. But that was just a gesture. I'm going to ruin that asshole's career, and I don't mean sometime in the distant future. I really am an agent, you know. I can—"

"Relax, Agent. I respect your professionalism, even if your partner doesn't. And you might still make a success of tonight. First, though, I want to know why you're interested in Charlie Victor." And just to show her how trustworthy I was, I put the .380 in my back pocket.

"You talked about a trade. What do I get?"

"If your story makes sense to me, maybe you get Charlie's box."

"The one you said you didn't have?"

"That's not what I said. But in any case, how bad do you want it? Would it really hurt all that much to simply tell me what you're up to?"

"Why is it any of your business?"

"Jesus, you just don't give an inch, do you? He was my friend, okay? I want to find out why he was killed. And right now, you and your partner are the best suspects I've got."

She sucked in her lower lip and scowled at the ceiling for a moment. "All right," she said, finally. "I'll tell you what I can. We have reason to believe your pet homeless person was going to hire an assassin to kill the President."

"Jesus, Mary, and Joseph."

"That would be an understatement."

"Wouldn't that take an awful lot of money?"

"Not necessarily. There are plenty of people out there who will try it just for the thrill or the fame. And some will take any fee at all, just to show that they are professionals."

"Which they are not, in that case."

"Maybe not, but they're still potential killers. A lot of agents have died for assuming that nut cases can't also be deadly."

"You said you had reason to believe Charlie was lining up a hit man. What reason?"

"That's classified."

"Screw classified. I thought we were talking about a trade here."

"Somebody sent the President a threatening letter."

"Charlie?"

"No, somebody else. Somebody said they were fed up with the President's treatment of poor people, so they had decided to contribute to the frag pot that some homeless guy was keeping on him. The letter didn't give his name."

"Did the letter call it that? A frag pot?"

"Actually, it called it a frag *box*, as I recall. That's a new term, I believe."

"And the postmark led you here?"

"And the postmark led us here. And we talked to poor people and social workers and jailers and priests. And we talked to a lot of homeless people."

"And you killed a dog or two."

"We don't do that sort of thing, Mr. Jackson."

"Be cruel to animals?"

"Be cruel to anybody, out in plain sight."

"So who did?"

"That, I am not free to tell you."

"But you know, don't you?"

"I'm not free to tell you that, either."

"Thank you. What about the black Hummer, the one that's been following me?"

"Now you're being paranoid. We had a walking tail on you for a while. But a Hummer? Get real. Who would use a stupid, obvious vehicle like that for surveillance work?"

"That's the question, all right. Who would?"

"Not us, I can assure you. That's all you get. Now it's your turn."

"Okay, I buy at least some of it. Tell you what: I'll give you Charlie's box if you let me finish looking at the contents first."

"I want to be there when you do."

"Sure, why not?" I stood up and gestured to her to do the same.

"So where is it?"

"On the table in the next room."

"You son of a bitch!"

"That has been observed, yes. I have some single malt Scotch on the table, as well as the box, by the way. Can I offer you a drink?"

"You must realize I'm on duty."

"Of course you are. Yes or no?"

"Why not?"

What a remarkable evening this was turning out to be. I gestured Krause toward the dining room, and I went back to the kitchen to get another glass. But first, I went back to the hallway and picked up the phone.

"Still with me Anne?"

"Yes."

"Could you hear all that?"

"I might have missed a word or two while I was getting my tape recorder, but mostly, yes. I love it. I don't know how much of it I can publish, but I love it."

"You probably won't be able to hear us when we move to the dining room. I'll hang up now and call you again when I get done with my disgruntled agent."

"I'll be here."

Back in the dining room, I gave Agent Krause a cut glass tumbler.

"Ice?"

"Never."

"A woman after my own heart."

"I seriously doubt it."

"Do you have a first name other than Agent?"

"No."

Right. Agent Agent, then. She had let down her hair enough to tell me that she hated her partner, but if I thought that meant we were going to be friends, I could just forget it. In fact, it probably guaranteed that we wouldn't be.

I settled into reading the last of Charlie's ledger and finishing my notes. Sometimes she looked over my shoulder, but mostly she wandered around the room, looking at my things and putting a serious dent in the Scotch supply. At a glass case on top of my buffet, she paused overly long.

"Do you play, Mr. Jackson?"

"You're looking at the violin? No. The only thing I play is a pool cue. The violin is a gift from an old friend, a sort of memento."

"Really? I would have thought you would be musical."

"Why would you think that?" I didn't look up from the pile of papers.

"Well, music is mathematical, they say."

"They do say that, yes. What's your point?"

"Didn't your name used to be Numbers Jackson?"

I was glad my back was to her, because that was a real kick in the guts, and there's no way my face wouldn't have told her so.

"I can't imagine where you would have heard that," I said. And that was absolutely the truth. Numbers Jackson was actually the nickname of my Uncle Fred, not me. But that was still way too close to home. And how the hell had she found it?

"You know, this box really doesn't tell us anything about who the hired assassin was going to be," she said.

"If anybody," I said.

"Oh, there was somebody, all right. Or there will be. And I am going to find him. But of course, your friend Victor can no longer help me, so I need somebody else."

"Well, we all have needs." I started dumping all of Charlie's junk back into the box.

"Yes we do. And you and I are going to help each other with them. Because, you see, *somebody* is going to go down here."

"I assume you mean for the murder of Charlie Victor."

"No, Mr. Jackson, I mean for the conspiracy to assassinate a president, the case that I am going to get a commendation for solving. A commendation and a new partner. Do we understand each other quite well now?"

So there it was. Find the hit man or invent one, because Agent Agent said so. And Agent Agent also knew a name from my blighted past in Detroit and maybe a lot more. Worst of all, I had foolishly hung up the phone, so I had neither a witness nor a recording of the extortion. So as much as it galled me, I would have to play by her rules. I gave her a silent nod, just in case she had some kind of recording device of her own. Then I put Charlie's box in her hand.

"Don't forget to pick up the magazine for your gun on your way out," I said.

"Thanks for the drink." She smirked and left.

There was a time when her threats would have seemed laughable. Not so long ago, either, but another era. Now we have the insultingly titled Patriot Act, and anybody who has read even a snippet of it and not been scared witless wasn't reading very carefully. As a bondsman, I knew all too well that it's an extremely fine line that decides which side of the law you are on. And if you have no rights, that's very, very bad, because all too often, the law is enforced by the Agent Agents of the world. And besides not getting their facts right, they have no more professional integrity than a pack of hungry wolves. I had thought she was annoying. Now I knew she was downright scary.

I stood at the front door and watched her drive away in a featureless government sedan, then reset the door alarm and called Anne Packard back and gave her a short version of the encounter.

"Did you get enough notes from the ledger for me to do a write-up, I hope?"

"I tried, anyway. I also got an address that my lady spook might not have noticed."

"Oh?"

"The box itself had what I thought at first was an importer's stamp on it. But when I looked closer, I saw that it was really drawn onto the box by hand, with a felt-tip pen or some such."

"Why is that important?"

"The address was in Mountain Iron."

"As in Mountain Iron, Minnesota?"

"The very one."

"Herman, I'm not inclined to think there are a lot of cigar importers on the Iron Range."

"Neither am I. I'm thinking it's either a place where Charlie had a stash, or the address of his father, which could be the same thing. I'm going to go have a look."

"When?"

"Tomorrow, early."

"I'm coming along."

Northland

Before dawn the next day I picked up Anne Packard in front of her office and we headed north in my BMW. She was dressed in professional woman's casual: slim-fitting khaki pants tucked into suede boots, a soft emerald green turtleneck sweater under a wool car coat, her usual thin, tailored leather gloves, and some tiny gold loop earrings. The earrings seemed to set off the gold flecks in her eyes, which I hadn't noticed before. The lady had style. She also had coffee and pastry in a white paper bag and an appropriate look of cheerful determination.

For the first thirty miles of I-35, we met a steady stream of headlights from inbound commuters. After twenty miles or so, she said, "Good grief, is it always like this?"

"Scary, isn't it? Apparently, life on your own little half acre up by Forest Lake or Scandia, with unleashed neighborhood dogs and strange snowmobiles in your yard and raccoons in your attic, is so wonderful that it's worth getting up at five every damn morning to follow somebody else's bumper for an hour or more. Personally, I don't get it."

"Sometimes it's nice being a newspaper person," she said, nodding. "It means you have to be aware of current trends, but you aren't allowed to judge them."

"I don't think I'm wired that way."

"No, you don't seem to be. So what was your idea of the golden age?"

"The what?"

"You know, the time when everything was right with the world? The time we ought to go back to? Everybody has one."

"Oh no, you don't."

"Excuse me?"

"I know you reporter types. You're trying to trick me into rhapsodizing about the good old days when cholesterol was good for us, nobody rigged elections, and a gallon of gas cost less than a small loaf of bread. Then you can give me some clever label, like 'pre-postmodern reactionary obstructionist,' and you won't have to think about who I really am any more. Not on your life."

She chuckled. "I usually try for something shorter than that."

"Like 'renaissance man,' maybe?"

"I was thinking 'curmudgeon.'"

"I'm not old enough to be a curmudgeon. How about post-renaissance man?"

"Have a doughnut. They're the postmodern low-cholesterol kind."

"Thank you, I will."

We had the northbound lanes pretty much to ourselves, but I stayed at just barely above the speed limit, figuring that with that much traffic in the southbound lanes, the State Patrol would have a presence somewhere nearby. Fifty thousand people, all driving bumper-to-bumper and too fast were bound to need some guidance sooner or later.

Finally, around the town of North Branch, the traffic thinned out to nearly nothing and the dirty gray sky started to get back-lit with something that passed for dawn. I poured some more coffee from my own Thermos, switched off the cruise control, and let the machine have its head a little, running a constant throttle rather than constant speed. The sprawling 'burbs fell away behind us, and we cruised into the land of black-green pine and cedar forests, with occasional tiny farms so poor, all they could raise were blisters and junked cars. The road behind us was empty. I increased my speed a bit more and settled into the rhythm of machine noise and passing landscape.

"Have you been up on the Iron Range a lot, Herman?"

"First time," I said.

"You're originally from...?"

"Iowa."

"What did you do there?"

"Not much."

"Married?"

"No."

"What made you come to the Twin Cities?"

"That's a long and not very interesting story."

"This is a long trip. Did you have some trouble back there?"

"Nothing worth talking about."

She laughed. "Wow, you don't give much away, do you?"

"No, as a matter of fact, I don't."

"Then why are you traveling with a newspaper person?"

"Because of Charlie Victor. I had this strange notion that he shouldn't just die on a sidewalk in front of a pool hall and get ignored, as if he had never even existed. I thought his story ought to be told."

"I can understand that. So tell me his story, then."

So I did. I told her how he always bought a bond from me in the fall and I told her most of his in-country stories from the jungle. I did not, of course, tell her how his being abandoned in the tunnels reminded me of a dumb kid running scared in Detroit. But I told her quite a lot.

"What about the fragging business?"

"Ah, yes. How could I have left that out?" I told her.

‹›‹›‹›

It took Charlie seven weeks to walk out of the jungle, a lot of which was spent hiding and all of which was spent being lost. He didn't know where his firebase was in the first place, so he didn't try to go back there. But he remembered when they were being choppered into the ville that they had turned above a river and then gone fairly straight the rest of the way. He figured if he could find that river, he could follow it downstream until it joined with some others, maybe even the Mekong, and eventually led to civilization. There were a lot of patrol boats out around the Delta, he had heard. If nothing else, he ought to be able to get picked up by one of them. He knew which way his platoon had come into the LZ. He left in the opposite direction.

He took all the gear and ammunition that he could carry, but he only had food and water for about two days. Water was the biggest problem. He had canteens, but no safe place to fill them, and he wasn't sure if he trusted his standard-issue purification tablets. He had heard about some kind of big tree that sent all the water from its branches down to its roots every day at sundown. You could hear it gushing inside the soft wood, the story went, and if you slashed open the bark, you could drink it.

Just before sundown on his third day, he made camp in a deep thicket of alien-looking trees in triple-canopy forest, and he slashed the bark of every different kind of tree he could see. He stayed awake all night long, listening, but he never heard any gushing and he never got a drink. The next morning, he saw that he had made so many slashes, he might as well have set up signs pointing to his camp. After that, he resigned himself to filling his canteens with paddy water or from puddles where he saw animals drinking.

He changed his attitude toward enemy patrols, as well. At first, he hid from them. Then he got to wondering if some of them might be just as careless and unmilitary as his own squad. So he followed a patrol during most of one day. When they settled down into a crude camp for the night, he snuck up and killed the sentry with his knife and took his food and water. He also took an AK-47 and a lot of ammunition. He figured if he had to get into a firefight, he didn't want the VC to be able to distinguish the sound of his firing or his muzzle flashes from their own.

It was a good strategy. Two nights later, he tried the same thing again but accidentally awakened one of the sleeping grunts. He wound up killing the entire squad with a couple of grenades and the stolen assault rifle. Things were definitely looking up. He joked to himself that as long as the VC kept patrolling the jungle, he could live there indefinitely.

At some level, though, he knew that if he kept it up long enough, the VC would mount an operation to hunt him. He had no idea how long that might be, but he tried not to dally in the jungle, waiting for it.

He fell into a routine. He traveled at night, hunting enemy patrols whenever he was out of food and water. During the day, he hid and slept, usually as high as he could get in some very leafy tree. But he never slept more than a couple of hours at one time, constantly waking up and rebriefing himself on who he was and what he was doing. He told himself he was a panther in combat boots, silent, deadly, and remorseless. He told himself he was young, fast, strong, and invulnerable. He told himself he was a legend, that the VC were afraid of him. He told himself a lot of things to keep from facing how wretched and alone he felt.

Eventually, he found the river. By then, he had contracted malaria, dysentery, and every kind of bug bite and body parasite known to the rain forest, which was a lot. Weak from dehydration and hunger, he built a crude raft and simply let himself drift downstream. After three days on the water, he floated into a backwater of the Mekong, where a firefight was in progress between three US Navy "Pibber" patrol boats and a small fleet of armed sampans. The Navy won, and Charlie was picked up with the rest of the flotsam.

He spent three weeks in a hospital in Manila, mostly getting his intestines rehabilitated. When he had first walked into the jungle, he was six feet, two inches tall and weighed a hundred and ninety-five pounds. When he was picked up, he weighed a hundred and forty, and he never again seemed to be able to stand straight enough to be over six feet. The Army gave him new uniforms, corporal's stripes, and a bronze star. Then they sent him back to his old platoon. Nobody in authority would talk to him about bringing court marshal charges against Lieutenant Rappolt.

Rappolt was still there, and Charlie might have been willing to forget about the whole abandonment episode, as happy as he was to be alive and not an FNG anymore. But the idiot leut kept harping on it. He told Charlie that he, by leaving him at the ville, had made him into a better soldier, had forced him to overcome his own inadequacies. He finally went so far as to tell Charlie he had made him into a man.

"Well, I sure do thank you for that, sir," said Charlie, as he plunged his K-bar knife under Rappolt's rib cage and up into his heart. "I probably couldn't have done this, otherwise."

Later that day he was burning his bloodstained fatigues in a honey pot when Bong, who was now also wearing corporal's stripes, brought him a big wad of money.

"I figure this is yours now, man."

"What is it?"

"The frag pot, baby. All of it. I was the official keeper. We been collecting on that asshole ever since you been gone and a long time before you even got here. Thanks, man. Anybody ever needed to die, it was that mufucker."

And that was how Charlie learned how the system worked. After that, he became the regular keeper of the frag pot. And he signed up for two more tours of duty, always with the stipulation that he could stay with his old outfit. He didn't quite understand why or how, but he felt as though he had inherited a duty to protect his squad mates from more Lieutenant Rappolts. And as luck would have it, there were several of them.

Iron Country

A hundred and sixty miles north of where we started, the inter-state freeway that had been steadily easing eastward made a more abrupt turn that way, plunging down into the Lake Superior basin to head for Duluth. I split away from it on Minnesota 33, through the town of Cloquet, following a sign that said "Range Towns."

What I expected to find there was not so certain. Charlie had said that he hated his father so many times that I had to believe it. But maybe hating him was not the same as not trusting him. The old man could still have been his banker. And in any case, the address on the cigar box did not get there by accident. He meant me to read it, of that I was sure. Time to find out if he also meant me to follow it.

North of Cloquet, the landscape turned open, rocky, and white. The lasting winter snow cover had already arrived, broken here and there by windswept outcroppings of black rock. The buildings got more run down and farther apart and the farm-steads disappeared altogether. We crossed the Saint Louis River and linked up with Trunk Highway 53, which headed straight north, four lanes with a wide center median, though it had lots of signs telling me it was not a freeway.

Anne had been napping under her coat, and now she poked her head out and looked around.

"Where are we?"

"Forty miles south of the town of Virginia. We're all out of coffee, I'm afraid."

"This is quite a road. It must have cost more to build than the total value of all the towns that it connects."

"Maybe there was more to connect, back then. Now, neither the road nor the towns look like much."

"No. And it takes fewer and fewer buildings to even qualify as a town."

"Three," I said. "I've been counting. Anything more than three, and it's a town plus a suburb."

"But there aren't a lot of those."

"No, there surely aren't."

To me, it felt like a good place to get away from, the kind of country that makes you appreciate a new set of rubber and a well-tuned engine. Because if your car ever died and left you to walk back to civilization, you could be in for one damned long trek across the windy steppes.

I put the pedal down a bit more and blasted past places with unlikely names like Zim and Cotton and Cherry. As we approached Eveleth, I could see a featureless pillbox called the U.S. Hockey Hall of Fame perched on a hilltop, standing guard over an abandoned two-story motel with weeds and scrub trees growing out of its pavement. I took the exit off the non-freeway.

"Is this it?"

"No, this is Eveleth. Charlie claimed to have killed a man here once, in a VFW bar upstairs over an appliance store. I thought I would just go and see if there is such a place."

"See if there's such a place as a cafe, while you're at it. Those politically correct doughnuts aren't staying with me very well."

"I'll look for a sign that says 'Bob Dylan ate here.'"

"Just look for a sign that says 'Open.' That's as much as you're likely to get on the Range."

She was right. Eveleth wasn't quite a ghost town yet, but the closed stores outnumbered the working ones by a big margin and the streets were almost empty of traffic. The only second-story bar we found was a BPOE, rather than a VFW, and it was over a union hall, not an appliance store. Both it and the hall looked closed. There was no sign of a Greyhound bus depot. Was that an indication, I wondered, of how close to reality Charlie's stories came?

We found an open diner on Main Street, where we sat and looked at stuffed and mounted fish, old license plates, and display cases of antique carnival glass, while we ate "world-famous Taconite Burgers" and "authentic Cornish pasties." They were surprisingly good. The pasties could be had "with or without," and I had to be told that the commodity being referred to was rutabagas. I had mine without and did not regret the choice.

The waitress, a pretty, self-conscious girl who didn't look to be more than nineteen, didn't know where the bus used to stop, but she did know that the appliance store on Main Street used to have something else upstairs before they had a fire.

"That was back before I was born," she said.

Things were looking up.

The cook, an aging black man who must have overheard our conversation, stuck his head out of the kitchen.

"The bus used to stop at the big front porch on the hotel, a block over east," he said, pointing. "Not no more, though. The place ain't even a hotel no more, got turned into a 'partment building, years back. There wasn't nobody wanted to ride the bus no more, no how."

"Did you come here on that bus?" said Anne. She took his picture.

"You're a smart lady. Yeah, I come here on that bus. Got off at that hotel in nineteen and fifty-two. Lots of jobs down in the Cities then, but you had to come a long ways north before it wasn't still the South, if you know what I mean."

"We know, believe it or not," I said. Anne gave me a look of surprise.

"Yeah? Anyway, so I come here and I been flipping them burgers ever since. Now I suppose you'll be wanting to know where Bobby Zimmerman grew up before he got to be Mr. Hotshot

Bobby Dylan and picked up some kind of accent ain't nobody on the Range or anyplace else ever heard before."

"Actually," said Anne, "we couldn't care less."

"I was right; you're some kind of smart lady." He grinned broadly while she took one more picture of him.

〈〉〈〉〈〉

I pulled back onto the highway and headed north again, checking my mirrors as I got back up to cruise speed. There was nobody behind us. Ten miles later, the road curved left to swing around the southwest corner of Virginia, which looked as if it might actually be a real city. I cruised up a big hill on its west side, ignoring the signs for skiing areas and mine tours, and took the exit for Highway 169, westbound. My next stop should have been Mountain Iron. If it was still there.

It was a diamond interchange, with a stop sign at the end of the ramp.

"Apparently we have to choose between new and old Highway 169," said Anne. "On your map, I don't see that distinction."

"The new one looks like some more of the same wide, four-lane, non-freeways they have here. I'd be willing to bet it wasn't even there when the address got written on the cigar box. I say we take the old road."

"Spoken like a true investigative reporter."

"Which I am not. That's why I have one with me." But I took the old road, all the same. We left the fringes of Virginia behind us very quickly and settled into a sedate fifty-five miles an hour on a narrow, two-lane highway that was built following the path of no resistance, making wide curves to avoid rock formations and gullies. Six miles out, it made a particularly sharp s-curve. A few dozen simple box-like buildings clustered around the road in crude rows, as if they had all fallen off the back ends of trucks that took the curve too fast. Since then, they had not been fixed up. I would have said they were all abandoned, except that some of them had smoke coming out of rusted tin chimneys.

"I think we have arrived at Mountain Iron," I said.

"How can you tell?"

"It has a little bitty water tower and a post that used to hold up a stop sign. If that's not civilization, I don't know the stuff. We're looking for Third Street."

"This place doesn't look as if it ever had three streets, and I mean back in its boom days."

"You think they had boom days here?"

"Well, maybe an eventful afternoon now and then." She had the tiny silver camera out again and was shooting as we drove.

The street signs were infrequent, to say the least, and were as badly rusted as the chimneys, but we found one that said Third and turned down a street that had exactly six tiny houses on it before it quit at a big pile of rocks and some stunted pine trees. I made a U-turn at the rock pile. Charlie's father's house, if that's what it was, was the last one in the row.

It was maybe twenty-four by twenty feet, tops, with asbestos shingle siding in an indescribable color and a covered porch with empty flower boxes on the rails. There was no smoke coming out of the chimney, but there were vehicle tracks in and out of the unshoveled driveway. Out in the back yard, half covered by snow, there were a couple of plastic lawn chairs and a barbeque made out of half a steel drum.

Next to the house was an ancient pickup, so rusted that its fenders wiggled in the light wind. It had tracks going to it, but not fresh ones. On the rear bumper were a couple of faded stickers that said "UNION WORKER AND PROUD OF IT" and "BAN IMPORTED STEEL." I thought that was hilarious, considering that the truck was a Toyota.

"Chez Victor," I said. "White tie optional." I pulled up at the place where a curb might be buried, if there were any.

"You're not going in the driveway?"

I shook my head. "That set of tracks is from some kind of vehicle with big tires and a lot of ground clearance. If I try to go in there, my undercarriage will bottom out on the snow and we could spend the rest of the day trying to shovel it out."

"Do you have a shovel?"

"No."

"Good call, Herman. Park in the street, every time."

The snow turned out to be mid-calf height, and by the time we got to the front porch, my sixteen-fifty shoes were candidates for the trash bin. There was a doorbell button next to the door, but it was hanging away from the wall by its wires, so I pounded on the door instead. Then I shaded my eyes and peeked in through the tiny glass.

"Anything?"

"There's a light on in there, but I can't see anybody moving around." I pounded again, waited twenty seconds, then tried a third time.

"Maybe he's in the study, working on his rare book collection," she said.

"Books are probably all rare in a town like this. I think more likely, he just doesn't want to talk to anybody. A lot of old people turn into hermits. Let's have a look at the back door."

We slogged through more of the deep snow, past the pickup and around to a porch that was smaller than the front one and had no roof over it. The combination screen-storm door was swinging in the wind, its spring broken or disconnected. The door and jamb behind it had both been badly gouged by some kind of heavy tool. Again, I shaded my eyes and peered into the gloom.

"Well, he's there," I said.

"So, aren't you going to knock?"

"Do you have your phone handy?"

"Of course. Why?"

"See if you can get us a local sheriff of some kind. I think Charlie's father is sitting in a kitchen chair, with his head half on the table in front of him."

"What do you mean, his head half on the table?"

"I mean somebody blew his brains out."

"Oh. Oh, dear Jesus." She fumbled in her purse, then began punching buttons. I squinted to see better through the dirty glass. The light was pretty poor, and the line of sight wasn't the greatest, but I could definitely see an ace of spades in the dead man's hand. It looked as if it had been stuck there after he had died, just for somebody like me to see.

The Law of the Range

The sheriff was a collection of middle-aged sags and bulges squeezed into a heavily starched, too-tight uniform. He also wore cowboy boots, a Smokey Bear hat, and about thirty pounds of weaponry and gear. His name was Oskar Lindstrom, and he seemed as much in denial as in charge.

"You know, for a long time I thought I was going to retire from this job without ever having a murder to handle."

"That's really too bad." *I'm sure the murderer did it just to spite you.*

"We got a coroner in Virginia, don'cha know, but if I want a crime scene crew, I'll have to either ask for help from Duluth PD or call the BCA, over to Bemidji."

"I think you ought to have a crime scene crew, Sheriff." *Do I have to make the call for you, too?*

"Well, yeah, I guess so. I'll maybe just have a preliminary look myself, though, anyhow. You said you and your wife were here to see the victim?"

"She's n…" Anne stomped on my instep, hard, and gave me a penetrating look with a tiny shaking of her head. I didn't know if her pantomimed "no" applied to telling the sheriff she wasn't my wife or telling him she was a reporter, so I did neither.

"She's what, you say?"

"Excuse me," I said. "I tripped on the step, there. I was going to say she's just along for the ride, Sheriff. I came here to tell Mr. Victor that his son is dead."

"You call him Mr. Victor? Hell, he wasn't anybody special."
He put on a pair of leather gloves before trying the doorknob.
The door swung away from him easily, without needing the
knob turned. He walked into the tiny kitchen, stomping snow
off his fancy boots, and I followed.

"I don't know his first name. The street address was all I had."

"Jim. Or James, I guess. His name was James Victor. I've
known him all my life. He was an asshole, I don't mind saying.
The kind of guy would pick an argument with a post, just to
stay in practice. And now he's messing my life up again, giving
me a murder case. So, you couldn't leave notifying him up to
the authorities, then?" By which he clearly meant himself.

"His son was a homeless man. I'm sure the police have no
idea who his next of kin was."

"So that's what became of him, huh? Turned into a bum?
Doesn't surprise me, I got to say. But you knew where to find
his next of kin. Why was that, I wonder? And who the hell said
you could follow me into the house, here?"

"Oh, wasn't that all right? I'll be careful not to touch anything." Sure, I would. Anything I wasn't going to take, that is.
"I just thought we could all get in out of the cold."

"It isn't in out of the cold, just out of the wind. Looks like the
furnace hasn't been lit for some time. That half a cup of coffee
on the counter is froze solid."

The card in the dead man's hand looked identical to the one
they had taken off Charlie's body, but I was obviously not going
to get a chance to look at it closer. Meanwhile, Anne had her
little camera out and was holding it waist-high, partially hidden
by her purse, shooting everything in sight. Not that there was
much to shoot, other than the body. I couldn't tell if the rest
of the place had been trashed or if Mr. James Victor was just a
terrible housekeeper. Either way, it was a mess.

And so was he. There wasn't much left of his face, but what I
could see looked as if he had been beaten before he was shot. He
was also tied to the chair, and there was blood on the floor that
didn't look as if it had anything to do with the gunshot wound.

"Why was that, again, that you came all the way from down Minneapolis?"

"St. Paul, actually."

"Same damn thing. Now you've had time to think up an answer, so what is it, then?"

"I wrote a bail bond for Mr. Victor's son once, and I sort of befriended him. I figured if I didn't come and tell the old man, nobody would."

"You couldn't call him, then?"

"That would be pretty cold, Sheriff," said Anne. I liked that better than what I had been going to say. Obviously this was a woman who could think on her feet. She had put the camera away now and was easing her way back toward the door and making gestures that said, "let's blow this pop stand."

"Yeah, okay, I guess it would a been, at that. Now get on out of here. This is a crime scene, ya know."

"Happy to help out."

"Wait on the porch a minute, though. I need your name and address before you go. I would say 'don't leave town,' like they do in the cop movies, but hell, you can't hardly go across the street here without leaving town. That's a little joke, see?"

I smiled politely and gave him one of my cards, both of which seemed to make him very happy. I wrote my license number on the back of it for him, and he wrote "Mr. and Mrs." ahead of my name on the front. Then he shook my hand and gave Anne what might have been a salute, and herded us off the porch.

"Charlie said his father worked in the mines," I said. "I don't suppose you know what he did, exactly?"

"He's been retired for a lot of years now," said Lindstrom, crowding us further off the porch. "I think he used to drive truck, though. One of those big off-road monsters, you know? A Euclid or a Cat, or something."

"Oh really? So, not underground work, then?"

"You kidding? There haven't been any working underground mines on the Range for forty, fifty years. Used to be, you could take a tour through the main shaft of the first one, at Tower-

Soudan. But open pit was the wave of the future, don'cha know, except there's not even much of that anymore. The ones who cashed in their pensions before it all went to hell, like Jim there, they were the lucky ones. So what makes you ask, then?"

"Just curious." I tried for a nice, sincere-looking shrug. "Nice meeting you, Sheriff."

Back in the car, Anne said, "Do you suppose he really will call the BCA and get a proper investigation going?"

"I wouldn't bet on it. He seemed awfully glad to finally be left alone at the scene. You're in the newspaper business. Do you know anybody on the Duluth paper?"

"As a matter of fact, I do."

"Maybe you should call them up and give them an anonymous scoop. If our sheriff has press coverage, I'm sure he'll do everything by the book."

"I like it." She dug her phone out and started scrolling through some kind of list. "What was all that business about the underground mines, by the way?"

"There was hardly anything in James Victor's house that didn't look as if he got it at a rummage sale fifty years ago."

"I would agree. So?"

"So why did Mr. Victor, who never was an underground miner in the first place, have a shiny new pickaxe leaning against the wall in a corner of his kitchen?"

"I give up, why?"

"How soon do you have to get back to St. Paul?"

"Where are we going instead?"

"Tower-Soudan."

"Is that all one place?"

"I have no idea."

Night Life on the Range

I took Minnesota 169 back to the interchange on the west edge of Virginia and headed north again. I thought about going into the town to buy some hiking boots and some flashlights, but the day was already getting late, and I didn't know how much more of Anne's time I could burn.

"Why did you want to let the sheriff think we were married, by the way?"

"Did that make you uncomfortable?" said Anne. "I'm sorry."

"Not uncomfortable, just perplexed."

"If I had told him I was a reporter, then I'd have had to cover the murder story."

"I suppose you would have, yes. What would be wrong with that? I'd have waited for you."

"I'm not actually supposed to be here, is the thing."

"You said your editor told you to back off the story, knowing that you wouldn't."

"That was before. What he told me later, when I was filing my column, was to pursue it if I thought I just had to, but strictly on my own time. So if I admit I'm here, I have to take a vacation day."

"Do you have one to take?"

"I never seem to have any to take. I use them up as fast as they accumulate, nursing hangovers and working on the Great American Novel."

I looked over to see if she was putting me on. She gave me an open face and a palms-up gesture.

"A hard-drinking novelist? That's actually respectable, in some quarters. Do you shoot elephants and write about bullfights and wars?"

"No, I shoot pictures and write about bail bondsmen with mysterious pasts."

I shot her another look and was met by twinkling eyes and a mouth on the verge of a huge smile.

"Made you look," she said.

"Twit."

"Now tell me about Iowa."

"Never happen."

"Why?"

"It's too boring."

"You're a bad liar, Herman."

Maybe so, but I can stonewall with the best of them.

Tower-Soudan turned out to be two places. You come to Tower first, and if you blow right on past it because it's so small, you come to Soudan less than a quarter of a mile later. And to your amazement, you find that Soudan is even smaller. Somebody once told me that you can estimate the population of a small town by counting the number of blocks on Main Street and multiplying by one hundred. If that's true, then Tower had about three hundred people and Soudan didn't have any. But it had a big monument telling us we were in the right area.

The mine that Sheriff Lindstrom had talked about was on the north side of Soudan, and it wasn't nearly as closed-looking as he had implied. In fact, it had been turned into a state park. The skeletal framework of the pit-shaft hoist tower, unsheltered from the weather, poked maybe sixty feet up in the air, looming over an assortment of buildings and platforms and trails that meandered down a steep embankment.

The whole park complex looked bigger than the town on the other side of the road. A sign said that the underground mine tours were closed for a season just then, but there were lights on in the buildings, and the complex was obviously still staffed and open. As far as I could tell, the underground mine and a couple of open-pit ones beyond it were still in operation, even. I pulled into the outer parking lot, which was neatly plowed, and stopped but did not get out.

"I'm afraid I've dragged you off on a wild goose chase," I said. "I'm sorry."

"What were you expecting, Herman?"

"Something abandoned and boarded up. Charlie was an old tunnel rat. If he was going to hide a box of money around here, I figured he would pick a place that was underground. And I was hoping the new pickaxe was what he had used to break in, and we could follow the scratch marks or some such."

"I see," she said. "And where did his father fit in with all that?"

"Well, there was a gap or two in my theory yet."

"Hmm."

"I really am sorry."

"Well, it's not as though you're the first person who ever wasted my time. And I got the story of the second murder, anyway, for a tie in. Tell you what: find a place to buy me a dinner that doesn't include lutefisk, and we'll call it even."

As she spoke, the windshield began to get spotted with the first flakes of another snowfall. It wasn't exactly a blizzard yet, but it was enough to make the visibility rotten for the trip back to St. Paul. I sighed.

"Swell," I said.

"Looks nasty, doesn't it?"

"It looks like we're cursed, is what it looks like." I flipped on the wipers and switched the duct control to full defrost.

"Let's wait it out, then. We're far enough into the Range to get blizzards that can stop a sled dog. The world will not end if I don't get back until sometime tomorrow. I'll say I was covering the cranberry harvest in Brainerd, or something. You can use my phone to call your office in the morning, if you want."

"Does Brainerd have a cranberry harvest?"

"It does now. Look for a motel that doesn't predate the Second World War."

I sternly pushed aside the thoughts that were gleefully crowding into my consciousness.

"We're not going to find any four-star resort hotels, you know," I said.

"Then we'll have to find some other kind of attraction, won't we? Think like a reporter, Herman; learn to take advantage of what's around you."

Unbelievable, the straight lines people give me.

<><><>

We went to a little strip mall on the outskirts of Virginia, to buy a few things. I went into a drugstore and bought a throwaway shaving kit and a toothbrush, and Anne went I don't know where and bought I don't know what. Then we drove back to Eveleth and took adjoining rooms at a motel whose only commendable feature was that it was an easy walk to the place where we had eaten lunch.

If we were about to become lovers, we weren't admitting that to ourselves yet. And the more I thought about it, the worse idea I thought it was, anyway. Sooner or later, people who are physically intimate become intimate in other ways, too. And of all the people I could not let that happen with, a newspaper-woman was close to the top of the list. But that was no reason we couldn't have a nice dinner.

But then, she said it first. Even to myself, I'm a bad liar.

The snow was getting thicker by time we hiked back to the main street. The temperature wasn't really bitter, but the wind made it feel worse than it was. We hunched into our coats and hurried. Fortunately, it was only three blocks.

The cafe was a lot livelier than when we had last been there. A folding partition had been rolled back to open up a much bigger dining room, with a bandstand, a bar, and a small dance floor. We took a booth in a corner, and a cheery fortyish waitress whose nametag said she was Madge brought us menus.

"Friday night," she said, "so I guess you know what that means, then."

"Um," I said.

"Let me guess," said Anne. "The special is all-you-can-eat fish fry."

"You got it, honey. Beer-battered walleye. And the Paul Bunyan drinks until eight o'clock, of course."

We ordered drinks and studied the menus. Over in the opposite corner of the room, a trio with matching black slacks and embroidered vests was pumping out schmaltz. A tallish blonde played a button accordion, accompanied by a bearded guy with an acoustic guitar. The third member of the combo looked like a refugee from a sixties jug band. He played a washboard with an assortment of bells and horns attached to it and sang into a microphone. Out on the dance floor, a few couples were doing something that might have passed for a waltz.

"The pretzels are zalty, the beer flows like vine," sang Mr. Washboard, in a faux accent that was probably supposed to be German. "After sixteen shmall bottles, the band she sounds fine. Ve laugh und ve dance und ve haff a good time…"

To my amazement, they really didn't sound too bad.

"Do you dance, Herman?"

"Only after the aforementioned sixteen small bottles or so. And by then, I would probably just fall down."

"I could teach you."

"You could get very frustrated trying, anyway. Where did you learn?"

"Political rallies."

"Get out of here."

"No, it's true," she said, shaking her head. "My father was a state senator from northern Wisconsin. He'd go to fundraisers in roadhouses and dance halls in little towns out-state, and the party faithful would listen to speeches and drink beer and dance the polka. I was too young to drink, so I had to learn to dance. Otherwise, I wouldn't have had anything to do at all."

"Where was your mother all this while?"

154 Richard A. Thompson

"Sitting home, mostly, disapproving. She refused to go out on the campaign trail. I'm not sure if she thought it was immoral or just undignified. Sometimes I think she was a closet Methodist. But she loved my father deeply, so she just sulked a little and kept quiet about it."

"That's a nice story," I said, meaning it. "Does that somehow lead to a career in journalism?"

"Partly, maybe. I surely saw plenty of reporters doing it badly. But even when they were sloppy with their stories, they seemed about as independent as a person can get and still be drawing a salary. It looked like fun."

"How come you never went into TV news? With your looks and poise, it seems like a natural evolution."

She shook her head again, though now she was smiling and blushing a bit. "That's not real journalism," she said. "I guess when it comes to my profession, I'm a curmudgeon, too. In my world, you're just not an honest-to-god reporter unless you write for a paper."

The waitress brought us our drinks then, a gin and tonic in a huge old-fashioned soda-fountain glass for Anne and a Scotch with a short beer for me. She asked if we were ready to order, and Anne told her to bring us some munchies for now, onion rings and spiced bull bites.

"Is that okay?" she said to me.

"Sure. Just what us health-food nuts always order."

"I figured as much. So. Pay me back for my nice story. Tell me about your father."

I sighed. "You just never give up, do you?"

"Not me. Bulldog Packard of the Mounties."

I took a sip of scotch and tried to think what I could tell her that would be consistent with rural Iowa.

"I don't remember my father," I said, which was the truth. "My mother claimed he died in the Korean War, but I don't recall her ever getting a government pension check. I think he just split."

"I'm sorry for you. Did you blame yourself for that?"

"Not really. I didn't come to that conclusion until I was fairly old. When I was a little kid, I thought it was cool to have a father who was a war hero."

"Even though he was dead?"

I shrugged. "I had plenty of friends who wished their fathers were dead. They probably envied me."

"And your mother?"

"My mother." I took another sip of scotch. "What can I tell you about my mother? She waited tables at a blue-collar bar, where she was probably also one of the best customers. She put…"

I had been about to say she put me in an orphanage when I was eleven, but then I realized that small towns probably don't have orphanages.

"She put?"

"She didn't want me around. I spent a lot of time with my uncle, out on a farm."

"Was that nice?"

I thought about running the phones for Uncle Fred and finding that I had a lot of money.

"It was okay," I said. "It was interesting." And I was amazed to realize how much of what I had just told her was true.

"And you never married?"

"Well, I hadn't ever seen a marriage up close that worked, you know? I couldn't figure out why people wanted it. What about you? Your ring finger doesn't look like it's ever worn anything."

"I guess I never saw one that worked, either." But her eyes wandered when she said it, and she toyed with a phantom ring on her left hand, telling me the real story. I touched her glass with mine and gave her what I hoped was an understanding smile.

Our food came, and we laid into it. We liked it so well, we ordered more of the same, plus some stuffed potato skins, rather than what she called "an honest meal." And we had more drinks, of course. And after fewer than sixteen but more than I could easily count, she really did get me out on the dance floor. I don't know if the dance I wound up doing had a real name or not. But just as the singer over in the corner had promised, we danced and we laughed and we had a good time. She was an easy person to be with.

It was past midnight when we walked back to the motel, leaning on each other. The wind had died down and the snow had changed to puffy, floating flakes that actually managed to make the dirty old town look postcard-pretty. We indulged in a very chaste goodnight kiss and let ourselves into our respective rooms.

Running in the Dark

Our rooms had a connecting door, in case we wanted to call them a suite. I had no idea if the doors, one on each side, were locked, but I assumed so. The walls were paper thin, and through them, I could hear water running in Anne's room, presumably the shower. A cold one? I should be so irresistible.

Still fully dressed, I lay on the bed for a while and listened to the rushing sound, wondering if there was something I might have said to make my sexy journalist fall into my arms in an erotic swoon. Probably not. This was a very in-charge kind of woman, even back when she was busy trying to drink me under the table. If she had an incurable fever for me, I figured she would have come right out and said so.

It had been a long day and a surprisingly energetic and alcoholic evening, and I should have been ready to crash into oblivion, but I didn't feel even slightly like it. I got up and looked at the connecting door. The sound of the shower stopped, but no matter how long I looked at the door, it didn't open.

I sighed just a little, shrugged, and paced over to the windows. I pulled back a drape and looked idly out at the parking lot with its strange-colored sodium lights illuminating the falling snow. And froze.

A black Hummer had just pulled into the parking lot next to my 328i, and some large and dangerous-looking types were piling out of it.

They were dressed in black topcoats and dark slacks, like the big gatekeeper at Railroad Island, two nights ago, except that they also wore ski masks and carried some very heavy-looking firearms.

I went quickly over to the connecting door again, clicked open the deadbolt, and opened it. Almost instantly, I heard the bolt on the matching door in Anne's room click as well, as if she had been waiting there. She pulled it open a bit and I immediately shoved it the rest of the way and pushed her back into the room.

"Oh, that's romantic," she said. "Really charming. I think I may have made a big mistake here."

She was wearing some lacy, low-cut panties and the soft green sweater and quite possibly nothing else, and she nearly made me forget why I had opened the door. Nearly.

"We've got to get out of here."

"Why on earth?"

"And I really do mean *now*."

I shut the door and threw the deadbolt, then took her hand and pulled her into the bathroom, where I unlocked the small window above the toilet and began to push it up.

"Herman, have you gone completely insane?"

The window had been painted shut for a long time, and opening it was doable but slow.

"I mean, if this is your idea of how to—"

From next door, we heard the sound of breaking glass and a few seconds later, the eardrum-splitting bang of an explosion.

Anne immediately joined me in pushing on the window, and it slid the rest of the way up suddenly, with a crash and some clunking of jiggled sash weights. A few white flakes and a lot of frigid air blew in from the black rectangle. While I shut the bathroom door and wedged a soggy, folded-over bath mat under it, she climbed up and put her upper body through the window. And as much of a panic as I was in, I still had to admire the sight of her taut, shapely legs and round buttocks. I hoped I would live long enough to see them in better circumstances.

"I'm not sure I can do this, Herman."

"We don't have a choice. Hurry."

"But how do I land?"

"Any way you can." I gave her behind a very unkind push and she disappeared through the opening.

"Get clear!" I said. I grabbed a pair of thin foam slippers from the floor and threw them out the window, then dove after them. In the bedroom behind us, there was another explosion.

It wasn't much of a drop to the ground, but I remembered how fragile things like wrists and necks are, and I did a tuck-under on the way down and landed on my shoulder blades with only minor agony. Anne had used her hands to break her fall and was getting up slowly, nursing her left wrist. I put an arm around her waist and helped her up, then tossed the slippers in front of her.

"Step into those," I said, "and then let's move."

"Where?" She picked up the slippers, rather than putting them on, folded her arms in a protective gesture, and started to run where I pointed.

"Out to the alley first. It's been plowed clean, and we won't leave tracks."

We ran down the alley for fifty yards or so, past a jumble of garages and small outbuildings behind a block of houses. At a yard that had a cleared sidewalk in the back, we turned into a tiny fenced garden, ducked behind a corrugated potting shed, and chanced a look back.

Nothing. Nobody behind us. I was wishing I had taken a moment to grab my coat, and I could only imagine how cold Anne must be feeling. She put her slippers on, finally, but they can't have helped much.

Then we heard the snarl of an over-revved engine, and the Hummer came tearing around the end of the motel. It went to the far end of the alley and stopped, and two men with flashlights got out. Then the big vehicle sped down the alley, past where we were hiding, and let another man out at the opposite end of the block.

We were bracketed.

We ran through the back yard and around the house, just in time to see the big SUV cruise around the corner of the street, moving slowly now, checking out front yards with a spotlight. There was no way we had enough room to cross the street in front of it and not be seen.

"Back," I said, and Anne needed no further coaching. We ran back the way we had come and tried the side door on a garage.

Locked.

But the second garage we came to, larger than the first one, was unlocked, and I pushed it open, pulled her inside, and shut it as quietly as I could. The lock on the door had no turn button on the inside, so I looked around for something to block it shut with. By the light of my trusty Zippo, I found a big double-headed axe hanging on the wall. I rested the end of the handle on the floor and wedged the head into the crack between the jamb and the door. I stayed there and held it, just in case I hadn't wedged it tight enough, and gave Anne my lighter.

"Try to find another one," I whispered.

"Another axe?"

"Another thing that could be used as a weapon. Tire iron, pry bar, anything. But keep the lighter away from the windows."

She faded into the darkness and came back a short time later with a crowbar and a blade from a rotary lawn mower.

"Good job. You get first choice." She picked the crowbar.

"Herman, I'm scared."

"Relax, Anne. And keep your voice to a whisper. We're going to make it through this." I had absolutely no idea how.

The garage was not small, but most of it was filled with the massive hull of some kind of cruising sailboat.

"See if you can get up and inside that thing," I said, pointing. "If they break in, I'll try to draw them away."

"I can't ask you to do that."

"Now would be a good time," I said. "And quietly."

She gave me a soft kiss on the cheek, which I found totally surprising and rather touching, and disappeared into the dark interior.

We waited silently in the dark for maybe five minutes. I wondered how clear our footprints were in the new snow, then pushed it out of my mind as just one more thing I couldn't do anything about. Then something bumped against the outside of the garage, and I could dimly hear voices. The lock handle on the overhead door, by the bow of the boat, rattled. *Shit!* I had completely forgotten to check that one.

"This one's locked," said a voice.

Thank God for small favors.

"What about the man-door?"

"Checking it now."

Suddenly somebody on the other side of my wedged door was jiggling the knob.

I grabbed the mower blade in my right hand and held it over my head, ready to strike down on the first thing that came through the door. With my left hand, I held the axe in place. If somebody decided to shoot through the door, I was a dead man. Or through the wall, for that matter. The place really wasn't built all that solidly. Its only good feature was that it had only two very small windows, and they were set high off the floor, where an ordinary person couldn't look through them without standing on something.

The doorknob jiggled again and somebody pushed on the door at the same time. It moved maybe a quarter of an inch before the wedging action of the axe head took hold and stopped it. I resisted the enormous urge to push it back to where it had been.

"No joy," said the voice outside.

I heard another bump against the side of the garage, and I continued to hold the mower blade high, ready to strike with it. Then a couple of powerful flashlights turned the glass on one of the windows opaque yellow-white, while the beams swept around the interior, probing, accusing.

I abandoned my post by the door before the light got to it, diving under the boat. The hull seemed to be supported by some kind of a cradle, rather than sitting on a trailer, and there was barely room for me to squeeze under it. The discs of light continued to dance around, but they couldn't reach me. I forced myself to breathe normally, hoping to put myself into a state of calm control by some reverse body language. It didn't work. Some very old impulses were resurfacing. Very old. But I wasn't very old anymore. Suddenly I was fourteen again, and quite sure I was about to die.

The Chill Below

Michigan Central Station is the only building left standing in the center of Detroit's old downtown, other than the twin office towers behind it. The towers are vacant and abandoned now, the lower-level windows boarded up. The train station is still in use, but it looks like a derelict, too, surrounded on all sides by blocks and blocks of empty landscape, where all the buildings have been leveled and replaced with nothing.

I see it suddenly, as I break out from the alley between a bank and an insurance company building, still running. My lungs are on fire. I would tell myself to stop and take a few deep breaths, but that won't do it. I need a lot more oxygen than that. And I will need more yet. I put my hands on my knees and bend over for a moment, resisting the urge to puke. Then I straighten up and move on.

I can clearly see the station now, but there's no way I can get to it. The space between it and me is full of cops, guardsmen, and rioters, all beating the shit out of each other. It looks like a battle scene from the Trojan War, only with firearms and smoke canisters.

Over near the terminal building itself, there is a beat up car beginning to catch fire back by the gas tank. It looks just one hell of a lot like Jerp's Mercury.

Forget about the troops. Forget about catching your breath. You can get through, somehow. You have to. Jerp could still be there. But even as I start running, I see the flames spread.

Then the gas tank blows, lifting the ass end of the car six feet off the ground.

What the hell do I do now, besides try again to catch my breath? Get someplace else, anyplace else. Not back downtown. I just came from that way, and it's no good. Run. Move, damn it!

Away from the terminal building, toward the river, three or four sets of train tracks bend away from the main lines and disappear into a black tunnel, plunging down to go under the Detroit river. Nobody in his right mind would go there on foot.

So I do.

Maybe twenty yards into the tunnel, stumbling over rocks and railroad ties that I can't see, I find a string of freight cars, just sitting. The doors all look shut, so I climb under a car and scrunch up behind one of the big wheels. Clutching my baseball bat, the only protection I have besides my young, fast legs, I hug the track ballast and pray that I won't be seen.

Stay here, stay here, stay here. Wait this thing out.

I stay until the sun goes down and the urban battlefield behind me is empty of people, lit by the occasional burning car or trash fire. Even in a real war, people eventually get tired and go home, I guess. Walk back over and check the Mercury for Jerp's body. Nope, empty. Well, that's something.

Suddenly I remember that my pad has been torched. Where to go? Where to spend what's left of the night? Where to sleep? God, I need some sleep.

Six-by-six Army trucks with fifty caliber machine guns mounted on them are patrolling the streets now. There's probably a curfew, and the troops are spooked and strung out, shooting anything that moves. And here and there, people who aren't so easy to see are shooting, too.

Back to the tunnel, is all I can think of. My freight train is still there, but I no sooner get under it than it starts moving, filling the dark with clanking, screeching noises. There's no place else to go, so I flatten out and let the train pass over me. Nothing hits me, so I guess there's more room than I had thought. I don't care what Uncle Fred says; if I get out of this alive, I'll never go collecting without a sidearm again. After the train is gone, I go deeper into the tunnel, clear down to where I imagine I can hear the river rushing overhead. There are more trains, later, but they don't frighten me anymore. I'm busy listening for other things, waiting out the night. And feeling very frightened and very, very ashamed.

⟨⟩⟨⟩⟨⟩

"Herman?"

And quite suddenly, it was over. Really over. Its power was gone, and not because Anne had called my name, but because somewhere deep in the back of my psyche, the right machinery had finally clicked and I knew I could redeem myself by my own hand. I had come a long way since Detroit, dragged myself up to adulthood and self-sufficiency with no help from anybody. And the terrible memory of that boiling summer had been easy to push away, never to be looked at again. But Charlie Victor's death had brought it back and it made me see, finally, the link between us that I hadn't been able to put a name on. Charlie had been abandoned by his comrades-in-arms. And to my shame, I had been an abandoner of another comrade. Sooner or later, I had to atone for that. I decided it would be sooner.

"Herman?"

The flashlight beams were gone, and Anne was leaning over the gunwale above me.

"Herman, where are you?"

"Keep your voice down. We don't know if our new friends are completely gone yet."

"Okay, my voice is down. Come and see what I found."

I dragged myself out and up and took the object she was holding out to me. It was a double-barreled shotgun.

"I don't believe this," I said. "Is it loaded?"

"I think so. There's some kind of shells in it, anyway, but I didn't pull them out to see if they were live. I was afraid I might drop them and loose them in the dark. I didn't find any extras."

I cracked the breech and carefully pulled out one shell. It was about the right weight and had a closed end, so I pronounced it live. I put it back in and snapped the weapon shut again. Suddenly I had a whole world of options.

"Can you see out the garage windows from up there?"

"They're awfully dirty, but I'm up high enough, yes."

"How did you get up there?"

"There's no ladder, but there's a sort of step thingy by the rudder that works pretty well."

I found the thing she was talking about and hoisted myself aboard as quietly as I could. The garage windows were dimly lit from outside by a single streetlamp in the middle of the block. I saw no silhouettes of anyone looking in. I leaned out a bit farther and saw parts of an empty alley.

"We need to find out if they've really gone."

"How about if we curl up together in the cabin of the boat and get warm for a few hours first? No, make that a few days."

"We have to know."

"And how do you suggest we find out?"

"I'm going back outside."

"I was afraid you'd say something like that."

We agreed on a secret knock, and Anne secured the door behind me. I immediately ducked into a shadow and began to work my way down the alley. I tried to move like a commando looking for a sniper, grabbing cover wherever I could, keeping my eyes moving, always pointing the shotgun where I looked. Nobody.

I hugged the shadows, forcing myself to take my time. Across the alley from the bathroom window that Anne and I had bailed out of, I hunkered down behind a garbage can and looked and listened.

The window was dark. It should have still been lit. I watched the snow drift silently down in front of it and it suddenly occurred to me that it was the most beautiful thing I had ever seen. Here I was facing almost certain death, and I was thinking that the snowfall in an alley behind a third-rate motel was the stuff of picture post cards. I almost laughed. And somehow I knew that now I could do whatever it took to survive. Or at the very least, I could save her. And that would be good enough.

I looked for movement or light in the window, the glow of a cigarette, the green spillover from a night-vision scope. I listened for a careless bit of chitchat or a scuffling footfall. I breathed deeply and counted my breaths. After thirty, I finally decided there was nobody there, and I moved on.

I wondered if the intruders had killed the night manager at the motel before they came for Anne and me. When I came to a spot across from the end of the motel, I broke cover and ran as fast as I could across the alley, flattening myself against the back wall. I risked a quick look around the corner, then a longer one. Again, I saw nobody. I turned the corner and moved along the end wall of the building, shotgun shouldered and up.

And quite suddenly, the jig was up. Four men in black came ambling around the corner, carrying their weapons loose and low, talking with each other, not looking at me. I cocked both hammers on the ancient shotgun, and they froze and looked up. And again, I knew I could face death and not blink.

"The first one of you who raises his weapon, gets his head blown off." I was surprised at how steady my voice was.

"You seem to be a little light in your math skills," said the one in the right center slot. But he kept his weapon where it was and with his free hand gestured to the others to do the same. He seemed to be the one in command, and I aimed the shotgun squarely at his head.

"Not really," I said. "I have two shots and there are four of you, and that's way too bad. It means I can only kill you and one other guy before the others drop me. But I can do that, and I will." God, I loved that voice. Hell, even I believed that voice.

But would he? He and the others were backlit by the spillover from the parking lot floods, and I couldn't read their expressions at all. They remained motionless for what seemed like hours, and so did I. Finally the same man spoke again.

"I don't think you'll shoot anybody in the back. You win, for now. We're leaving. Let's go, men. Slow and easy." And still keeping his gun at sling-arms, he turned slowly on his heel and walked away from me.

After a skipped heartbeat or two, the others followed suit. I walked quickly backward to the corner of the building, to use it for cover in case it was all a ruse. I kept the shotgun leveled at them. But they kept on going. A minute or two later, I heard car doors slam and an engine start. When I ran over to a dumpster at the edge of the parking lot and ducked behind it, I saw the Hummer cruise out the driveway and on down the road.

I permitted myself to tremble. I avoided walking anywhere for a while, because I was sure my legs didn't have a bone in them. And as I leaned on the dumpster and stared off at the dark streets, I saw flashing red and blue strobe lights, first a long way off, then closing rapidly. The law had arrived.

Ships in The Night

My new favorite sheriff, Oskar Lindstrom, led the parade in his Explorer, followed by a couple of deputies in unmarked cars and then a fire truck. When they got close enough to have me in their headlights, I put the shotgun on the ground and stepped forward, away from it. The sheriff got out of his vehicle and squinted at me, as if he couldn't believe his eyes. He had his revolver out and up, but when he recognized me, he relaxed a bit and pointed it at the sky.

"Some folks don't seem to know when to get out of town," he said.

"It's that small town hospitality," I said. "You just hate to leave it."

"Yeah, I'm so sure. So you stick around and blow up a motel room, just to be doing something?"

"We didn't do it, we had it done to us. I'll tell you the whole story, but first I think we ought to go check on the motel manager. He could need medical attention." I walked toward the motel office with the sheriff at my side. The others trailed behind us. As we walked, I gave Lindstrom a quick version of what had happened. He put his gun back in its holster and walked with his hands on his hips, shaking his head a lot and scowling. He looked as if I had personally brought him more trouble than the entire rest of his law enforcement career.

"Well, I can't imagine anybody making up something like that," said the sheriff. "So who do you think these people are, then?"

"I have no idea."

"I think you have a lot of ideas. You just don't like sharing them."

I was starting to think he might be right. Maybe I knew a lot more than I thought I did. Or I was about to.

The motel manager had been gagged and tied up but was otherwise undamaged. Apparently it had been one of the other motel guests who had called nine-one-one. We checked our rooms next, and to my amazement, there was very little damage beyond the broken window and a couple of kicked-open doors. If the sheriff hadn't gotten a call from somebody other than me, I'd have had trouble convincing him there had been any explosions at all. *Concussion grenade*, I thought. *Not meant to kill, just to stun and shock.*

"So, is that your shotgun back there?" said Lindstrom.

"No. I borrowed it from a garage with a big boat in it. We ran away and hid there when the goons came."

"That would be Elmer Carlson's garage. He's a retired carpenter, built that boat from scratch. Used to be, when his wife was alive, it was his place to go get away from her. He'd go out and pretend to work on the boat and then get drunk and pass out. She's been gone for a long time now, died of cancer, and he's confined to a wheelchair, has a nurse look in on him a couple times a day. So there's probably been nobody in the garage for years now. I'm surprised it wasn't locked. Where's your wife, then?"

I nodded my head in the general direction of the alley. "Still hiding in the boat. I have to take her some clothes."

"Well, I think maybe we're done with you here for now. Take your time. Have a shot of old man Carlson's booze, if you find it. He'll never be back out there. See me again before you leave town, though, hey?" He gave me a card.

"Sure, no problem."

I grabbed up everything from both our rooms and headed back out to the alley. Along the way, I picked up the shotgun again.

<>><>

It took Anne a while to respond to our secret knock, and for a brief moment I wondered if she had been attacked by a fifth member of the patrol, if that's what it was, while I had been drawn away.

But the third time I knocked, I heard the axe being pulled out, and then the door opened away from me. When Anne saw I was alone, she put down the crowbar and hugged herself again.

"Are you okay?" I said.

She nodded. "I was back in the boat again, and I wasn't sure I ought to come out. The question is, are *we* okay?"

"Yes. Anyway, we're clear for now," I said. "The bad guys are gone and the—"

"How can you be so sure?"

"Because I pointed my trusty shotgun at them and they got in their car and left."

She gave me her penetrating, skeptical stare again. I gave her what was probably a goofy-looking grin and nodded my head. "Yeah." I laughed at the sheer wonderfulness of it. "Just like that. I couldn't believe it, either. They ran off just before our friendly sheriff showed up. He's back at the motel now. I brought you your clothes. Maybe you'd like to—"

But instead of taking the bundle out of my hands, she wrapped her arms around my neck and kissed me long and hard. I pushed her back for a moment, just so I could put the shotgun out of the way, then kissed her back. Wonderful, euphoric stuff, escaping from mortal danger. Just about the best aphrodisiac there is.

"You're running on adrenalin afterglow," I said. "You should—"

"Come and see what I found," she said, still ignoring her clothes, though she should have been turning blue by now. She took my hand and led me back to the transom of the boat. We climbed aboard, then stepped down into the cabin.

"There's power," she said. She flipped a switch and a tiny light came on in the overhead. There was also a small electric space heater on one bulkhead, and she turned it on.

The cabin was small, but cleverly laid out. The entire bow of the boat was one big, triangle-shaped bed, upholstered in some kind of red plush fabric. Farther toward the stern, there was a bench seat and a fold-down table and a lot of shelves and mesh slings, with various kinds of gear in them. On one shelf, there was a case of beer in long-necked bottles and a quart bottle of Canadian Club.

"I don't think I want to go back to that motel room just yet, Herman."

"We probably shouldn't. If the nasties come back, that's where they'll look for us, not here. And we have more or less official permission to stay in the boat."

"Really? How did we get that?"

"The owner is a shut-in. The sheriff gave us his blessing to mess around in the garage."

"Mess around. I like that." She pulled the cap off the whiskey bottle and took a slug, then held it out to me. "Buy you a drink, sailor?"

"I don't think you want to be doing that," I said. "You're just a bit on the emotionally fragile side right now, you know."

"True, true," she said. She put down the bottle and wiped her mouth on her sleeve. Then she reached farther back on the shelf and picked up something small.

"Forget about the booze, then. Look at what else I found." She put it in my hand. It was a condom in an unopened wrapper.

Considering what the sheriff had told me about the owner of the boat, there was no way I believed Anne had found it there. She had to have bought some at the mall in Virginia and put one in the elastic band of her underpants. There was also no way I was going to tell her I knew that. Not for the first time, I marveled at my utter inability to read a woman, and I was grateful that Anne hadn't had the same problem with me.

Her mouth found mine again and this time, I did not push her away, even slightly. I put my hand under her sweater and pulled her against me, then laughed in spite of myself.

"What are you finding so funny, there, Iowa Jackson? I'll have you know I've been—"

"Your rear end is cold."

"Oh, that." She chuckled quietly. "Well, I wonder why? I'm cold all over, you know?"

"There's a cure for that." I pulled down the collar of her sweater and nuzzled her neck.

"Well for God's sake, let's get to it, then." She unbuttoned my shirt and, I swear, climbed inside it with me. Then she wrapped her legs around my torso and we traveled to that place that has heat and resonance and intensity but no name. Somebody once said that when you make love, the dogs don't bark. Time doesn't exist and neither does fear. I hadn't been to that place for a very long time, and it was nice to be reminded.

‹›‹›‹›

Much later, we treated ourselves to a drink of whiskey and a can of cashews that we found on another shelf. It was warm in the cabin by then, even hot, and after a nightcap and a snack, we made love again, much more slowly this time, savoring it all. Then we curled up together and slept the long, blissful sleep of people recently delivered from death.

I have to say Elmer Carlson had built himself a damn nice boat.

The Morning After
the Night Before

Dawn came with real sunlight, for a change. It streamed into the high east window and bounced around the garage a little before finally finding its way into the boat cabin. That made it dissipated, but still friendly.

The little space heater had been running all night, and the cabin was now much too warm for comfort. I stepped out into the rear cockpit and enjoyed the feel of the frigid air on my body. I looked at my watch. Only a little after eight. All things considered, it wouldn't have surprised me if we had slept until noon. A heavy hangover wouldn't have surprised me, either, but as far as I could tell, I didn't have one and wasn't going to get it. Never underestimate the curative powers of adrenalin and sex. Either one or both.

Anne was still asleep, and I grabbed my clothes out of the cabin and dressed in the cockpit. Then I went back to the motel to retrieve my car and get us some coffee from the lobby. The motel clerk did not seem to be my friend anymore.

"I could charge you for the damage to those rooms, you know."

"I get attacked in your motel, and you want to charge me for the experience? You're lucky I'm not a lawyer."

"Um. You're not, are you?"

I shook my head and gave him a reassuring smile. I was feeling much too good to get sucked into an argument, and anyway, he was looking more confused than angry. Obviously, nothing in his two-year community college degree had prepared him for this kind of incident.

"Did you call your insurance people?" I said.

"Sure, right away."

"And you're not hurt and neither is anybody else and you will be getting a police report to substantiate what went on, right?"

"I guess."

"Sure, you will. So relax. You'll have a good story to tell down at the corner saloon."

"I don't go to those places."

"Right. Me either. Tell you what: give me four cups of coffee and a cardboard box to carry them in and we'll call everything square."

"And then you'll go, right?"

"And then I'll go." Nice young man, but he really needed to do something about all that negative thinking.

I put the coffee on the roof of my BMW, took a flashlight out of the trunk, and lay down in the new snow long enough to check the undercarriage for bombs or bugs or other assorted bits of unwanted baggage. Seeing nothing amiss, I brushed myself off, got in with my coffee, and fired it up. Going around the corner of the motel into the alley, I punched the gas and did a short power slide, just for the pure joy of it. Then I went more sedately the rest of the way and stopped by the garage in the middle of the block, to collect Anne.

She was dressed by the time I got there, but still in the boat. We popped the lids on two of the coffees and sat with our feet hanging over the gunwale, eating Elmer Carlson's cashews and getting ourselves recaffeinated.

"Well, Herman, now you know my worst secret."

"I do?" I shot her a quick sideways look. "And what might that be?"

"What I look like in the morning."

I looked again, a little more critically.

"If that's the darkest secret you've got, I would say you have nothing to worry about."

"Well, you would say that, wouldn't you? Whether it was true or not."

"Damn right I would."

She chuckled and took another handful of cashews. They went surprisingly well with the coffee.

"I don't suppose we can go back to the motel and use the bathroom and clean up a bit?"

"As a matter of fact, we can. The clerk was so happy to see me go that he forgot to get our keys back. And anyway, it's not as if he's going to rent the rooms out again right away, with two broken doors."

We shut off the lights and the heater, and Anne wrote a thank you note and stuck it in the empty cashew can. On the way out, I bent a piece of wire I found hanging on the wall into a crude lock pick, and I used it to lock the door behind us. After all, who knew what sort of riff raff might be wandering in?

We drove back to Anne's room, since that was the one that still had all its glass intact, and while she disappeared into the bathroom, I used the bedside phone to call Agnes and tell her I'd be back in the office sometime in the afternoon.

"Is she cute?"

"I can't imagine who you're referring to, Aggie."

"Oh, good. She is cute. I'm glad for you, Herman."

"I don't know why you always think—"

"Wendell called, by the way." She always refers to Wilkie by his real first name. "He says he's got something for you. And a Detective Erickson from the SPPD called later. You want that number?"

"No, thanks. He made me wait. Now it's his turn. Anything else?"

"I, um, guess not. Not really." The energy had suddenly gone out of her voice altogether.

"Tell me, already."

"It's really nothing, Herman."

"Has that asshole Eddie Bardot been bothering you again?"

"He scares me, Herman. And that gets me mad at myself for being so silly, since he doesn't really do anything very threatening."

"What does he do, exactly?"

"Yesterday morning, he tried to leave an envelope full of money on your desk."

"What did you do?"

"I threw it out on the sidewalk. I told him he could pick it up or not, as he liked, but I certainly wasn't going to do so."

"Good move. So did he leave then?"

"He did, but later he came back. He hangs around. I think he only does it because he knows you're not here. He makes what he thinks are cute little sexual innuendos and says I should be nice to him because you aren't going to be around much longer."

"Does he, now? Next time he comes back, in fact the next time you even see him coming down the street, call Wilkie right away, okay? Tell him I said we need the trash taken out. I'll be back as soon as I can."

"Thanks, maybe I will."

"Not maybe. Do it."

"Drive safely, Herman."

"See you, Ag."

I hung up and dialed Wilkie's cell phone, but all I got was his voice mail. "I'm not here now, see?" said the recording. "So I can't talk to you. When I'm back, I will. You can leave a message, if you want to, and I might listen to it."

I waited for the beep and then left a message asking him to look in on Agnes. Meanwhile, Anne had come out of the bath. We left our keys in the room and headed out.

‹›‹›‹›

Sheriff Lindstrom's office was a new building just off the new Highway 169, not really in any town. His deputy gave us some coffee in real cups, and we settled into some visitor chairs in front of Lindstrom's desk in his inner office.

"I did a little write up of the business last night," he said. "Maybe you could look it over and sign it for me?"

"Sure," I said, and I began to skim through my copy. It was written in first person, as if it had been taken as dictation from me, so I felt free to edit it. When I came to references to Anne as my wife, I crossed them out and wrote in "girlfriend." That made me smile, and I wondered what she was writing on her copy.

"By the way, Sheriff, has your coroner determined when James Victor was killed yet?"

"Um, well, it's not so easy, you know. The heat turned off in the house, and all. Ah, why, ah, would you be wanting to know that?" He was visibly uneasy with the topic.

"Well, I was just thinking." I paused and looked into his eyes, and he did not hold the contact.

"Okay, then," was all he said. "You're allowed to think."

"I was thinking that if James Victor was killed more than three days ago," I said, "then maybe the killer or killers came to the old man to find out where the kid was."

"Oh, like that. I see. That could be, I guess."

"I was also thinking that yesterday at the murder scene, and again last night, you were awfully nice to me. Not suspicious or authoritative at all."

"Hey, I'm a nice guy. Just ask Marty out there."

"He's a nice guy," said the deputy from the desk in the front office.

"Sure you are. But I think you also knew you didn't have to suspect me of any wrongdoing, because you knew you had already seen the real killers."

"Just what the hell are you saying?"

"They came here, didn't they? To ask how to find old man Victor. And of course, you told them."

"Well, why wouldn't I? Not that I'm saying I did, mind you. That doesn't mean I had anything to do with—"

I held up my hands and shook my head. "I wasn't implying anything of the sort." I signed his report and pushed it back across the desk to him. "People ask for directions, you give them some. Nothing wrong with that. What did they say, that they were old army buddies, trying to get a line on Jim's kid?"

"You're pretty damn smart, you know that? You want a job as a deputy?"

"Hey!" said Marty.

"Yeah, they were here. I guess it can't hurt anything if you know that. They had an address for old Jim, but they couldn't find the whole damn town of Mountain Iron, they said. You wouldn't believe how much of that I get."

"Yes, I think I would. And you say they also asked about Jim's son?"

"They asked, but I didn't have anything to tell them. I'm thinking Jim didn't, either. One time he bitched to me about how his kid only sent him one lousy postcard in the last twenty years. He knew it was sent from St. Paul, but that's about it."

"Really? Did you tell them that?"

"Hell, no. I didn't like them. Bunch of arrogant, pushy types, acted like they owned the world and everybody should kiss their asses. So I didn't feel like telling them diddly."

"So when did James Victor die?" said Anne, also pushing her report form across the desk.

"It's iffy, like I said. The coroner says he could have died as much as a week ago. The guys who came here were five days back. Happy? Now, have you two got anything else to tell me? Like maybe who these guys were?"

"I wish I knew. They seem to be tied to Charlie Victor's past in Vietnam somehow, but they're way too young to have been there when he was. And they seem to be military, but I don't think they're part of any kind of actual operation, even a rogue one. That's as much as I know, and I'm not even sure I know that." I got up and headed for the door. On my way, I said, "The police detective in St. Paul who's working on Charlie Victor's murder is named Erickson. You might want to give him a call."

"Another St. Paul smart guy? I can hardly wait."

"I really think he—"

"I'll call him, I'll call him. Are you gone yet?"

"Ciao," said Anne, and we were, indeed, gone. But we didn't head south just yet. We went back to James Victor's house.

◇◇◇

Yellow CRIME SCENE tape was wrapped around the entire house several times, and the site was full of tire tracks and footprints. Anne took a picture of it.

"Did you tell the sheriff we were coming here?" said Anne.

"Of course not. He'd have just told me not to."

"So now we can pretend we didn't know any better?"

"I was thinking more of getting in and back out fast enough that we don't have to pretend anything."

"That's a good plan. What are we looking for?"

"A postcard, with a twenty-year old postmark on it, the one Charlie's father bitched about. You want to stay in the car and play innocent bystander?"

"Not on your life."

The back door was still unlatched, and when I looked at it more closely, I saw that the strike plate had been completely ripped out of the jamb. I swung the storm door out as little as possible, and we managed to slip inside without breaking the plastic tapes.

Inside, the place was pretty much as we had seen it the last time, except that now, of course, James Victor's body was gone. I had been wondering how the cops were going to make the famous chalk outline of the body, since it had been sitting in a chair. To my disappointment, they hadn't even tried. Maybe they only do that in the movies.

The rest of the house was an even bigger mess than the kitchen. Drawers dumped, upholstery cut open, everything thrown all over hell.

"It doesn't look as though our crime scene techies were very neat," said Anne, and she took some more pictures.

"I'm thinking this is the way they found it."

"Our bad guys' handiwork?"

"It would fit." I had also noticed some possible bloodstains in the living room, which I had not pointed out to her, and I wondered if the pickaxe in the kitchen had been used for some purpose quite different from digging ore. The crime scene people had taken it, in any case.

In the bedroom, the threadbare mattress on an old brass bed frame had been slashed, dresser drawers dumped, and even the dresser mirror had been smashed, then spun around backward and the paper backing torn open. Shards of slivered glass crunched under our feet.

"I think we're a day late and a postcard short, Herman."

"Maybe, maybe not. Sometimes people trying to be intimidating get in a frenzy and don't look carefully." I rotated the broken mirror back to facing the correct way. And stuck in the frame, in places that still had pieces of glass left, were some ticket stubs from a movie theater, a menu from a pizza joint, a church program from some long ago Easter, and an old postcard.

"Hello," I said.

"Something?" said Anne.

"Could be," I said, pulling it out. "It almost looks *too* old, though."

"Let's see it. No, it isn't. It's one of those nostalgia replicas, like they sell at the History Center gift shop. It's meant to look like something from before World War Two, but it's really not."

"It looks like a picture of a downtown park."

"Kellogg Park, the way it looked back in the streetcar days," she said. She flipped the card over. It had Charlie Victor's signature and James Victor's address on it, but nothing else. No greeting, no request for money, no message of any kind. I squinted at the tiny printing in the upper left hand corner, telling us what the picture on the other side was.

"That doesn't say 'Kellogg Park,'" I said.

"No, it has the older name for it: Viaduct Park."

And my mind flashed back to that first day in my office, when Charlie had told me about his cardboard box "under the wye-duct."

"What's under this park?" I said.

"Under it? Second Street, I guess, or most of it. The whole place is built sort of like a double-deck bridge, with a sloping street below and a park up on top."

"And under the sloping street?"

"Some hollow spots where street people hang out, I think."

"And I bet they sing, 'Oh, I live under the wye-duct; down by the winny-gar woiks.'"

"What on earth does that mean?"

"It means we just hit pay dirt. Lets get out of here."

The Road to the Wye-Duct

The road back to St. Paul seemed shorter than it had on the way out, but maybe that was just because it was familiar now. We skipped our new old favorite restaurant in Eveleth and instead had a late brunch in Hinckley, at a place with a tin tree on a telephone pole for a sign. It had a cloud of bluish smoke coming out of the kitchen exhaust, and it smelled like hot cooking oil and burning beef. In other words, it smelled wonderful. Inside, it also smelled like coffee and fresh bread, and I knew we'd come to the right place. I had the house special stew and Anne had some kind of large salad, with greens that were freshly flown in from Mars, I think.

"How's the stew?" she said.

"It's famous. The menu says so."

"Well, then, what else is there to say?"

"Actually, it's very good."

"I'm glad. How was the sex?"

If I'd been swallowing, I would have choked. Instead, I laughed and said, "You just don't beat around the bush about anything, do you?"

"First rule of reporting," she said, shaking her head and grinning wickedly. "You don't find out anything if you don't ask."

"All right, then, Lois Lane, the sex was wonderful. Does this mean we're going to do it again?"

"If we're lucky. Now comes the time when it gets really, really good for a while, before it all starts to go south."

I shot her a surprised look and found that she was holding her coffee cup with both hands and staring off into space with a sort of dazed look.

"Why should it all go south?" I said.

"Because it always does."

"That's really—"

"You worry too much, Herman. First we get the good time, and if it's really good, it makes it all worth it."

I couldn't help but wonder what had happened on all those political fundraisers besides dancing the polka. Whatever it was, it must have been terribly sad. And I was sure I shouldn't ask about it.

"What about my story?" she said, blinking her eyes back into focus. "Do we know any more than we did yesterday, apart from the fact that the homeless guy had a father who was also murdered and some goons who look like they *might be* military have been chasing us?"

"We can speculate, is all."

"I'm a reporter from the old school. I don't let myself do that. You do it for me."

"First of all, now that I've seen them up close, I would definitely agree with our witch, Glenda—"

"It was actually Glinda, in the Oz stories."

"Are you going to let me speculate or are you going to correct a bag lady's personal mythology?"

"Speculate, Herman."

"Okay. So I agree that our thugs are military types. And Charlie was murdered by some kind of gang, so that would also make these guys our best suspects. But they're way too young to have been in Vietnam when he was. So why do they care what he did when he was there?"

"I give up, why?"

"I don't know yet. But my gut feeling is that everything that's happened so far is somehow tied to his time in the jungle."

"But we have no proof of that."

"Not a shred. Put that aside for a moment and consider something else. Two somethings. One is that if these guys had really wanted you and me dead, I, at least, would be."

"You don't think they were afraid of your big, bad shotgun?"

"Not for a minute. If I had been a real target, they'd have paid the price and taken me out."

"So what did they really want with us?"

"Could be they thought we had a line on Charlie's stash of money, but I think it's more likely they were just trying to scare us off."

"That plays okay," she said, "but we still need a reason."

"They haven't found the money yet. And until they do, they don't want to fold up the tent and go off to wherever they came from. So while they're hanging around, they would rather you and I quit poking into their affairs."

"Absolutely maybe," she said. "What's the other something?"

"Timing. They killed Charlie's father before him, and they killed him quick. I mean, they beat on him some first, but when they were satisfied they had what he knew, they shot him in the head. 'We're done with you now, old man. Bam!' No screwing around."

"But when they killed Charlie..."

"When they killed Charlie, they took their time. I'm thinking they maybe even told him they had killed his father first, so he could think about it while he died."

"That sounds like a crime of passion, not a treasure hunt."

"It does, doesn't it? It sounds like a blood feud. They meant to kill Charlie and his father all along, and the money was just a little sideshow, an unexpected bonus."

"'Blood Feud' is a good headline," she said, making a little frame with her hands. "'Blood Feud Has Roots in Vietnam War' is even better. But whose blood, besides the Victors'?"

"That's the question, all right. Charlie said he killed, or collected money for killing, several officers. Could one of them have had a buddy, a classmate from West Point, whatever? I don't know. I think we need some personnel records from Charlie's old outfit. Last known addresses, so we can talk to whomever is left of them, see what they know."

"I don't know if the Army would give those out to a reporter. Maybe if I pretend I'm writing a book… Hmm. No. I just don't know." Her face said that she did know, and she wasn't happy about her prospects.

"I know a sort of renegade hacker who could possibly steal the information," I said.

"You know some strange people, Iowa."

"This is undoubtedly true."

"One other thing bothers me: how did the goons find us at the motel?"

"I thought about that, too," I said, thoughtfully stirring my coffee. "They were following me the day before yesterday, but we didn't have anybody behind us when we headed north, and I checked the BMW for a homing device before I left town. So that leaves your cell phone."

"When I called the sheriff from Mountain Iron? So they homed in on the signal? That seems a little far fetched."

"If they had the right equipment, they wouldn't have to. Modern cell phones broadcast their position every time they're in use. All they had to know was your number, and they could have gotten that from my phone records."

"That would only get them to Mountain Iron. How did they get to the motel in Eveleth?"

"They cruised around looking for a 328i. There aren't a lot of them on the Range, you know."

"Like one?"

"Just like that."

The last of my stew had turned cold, and I let the waitress take it away and bring me fresh coffee and a piece of apple pie that turned out to be about two inches high and sprinkled with enough cinnamon and sugar to open a small bakery. Anne looked at it longingly.

"I'm sure they have more," I said.

"You're a vile seducer."

"I certainly hope so."

She signaled the waitress, pointed at my plate, and held up two fingers. The waitress smiled knowingly and went off to get another piece.

The pie was something to die for, but our dessert was interrupted by Anne's cell phone.

"Now you know why I don't carry one of those damned things," I said. She waved a hand to shush me, turned away and spoke quietly into the infernal device. It was a short call.

"My editor," she said.

"How thoughtless of him."

"You don't know the half of it. How fast can you get me back to my office?"

"Well, I think the 328i will do something like Mach oh-point-twenty-five. If there are no cops out and you aren't afraid of flying, I can have you back in an hour."

"In one piece, would be nice."

"For some people, everything has to be perfect."

I didn't bother to tell her that I had another reason for wanting to fly down the highway at a speed that was probably insane. Far back, almost out of sight, I had again spotted a black rectangle that could definitely be a Hummer. Our military gang was not done with us yet.

Echoes

I dropped Anne at the *Pioneer Press* building, put the BMW back in the ramp, and walked to my own office. I turned the corner onto my block just in time to see my friendly shakedown artist, Eddie Bardot, picking himself up off the sidewalk. He glared at me as I walked by but said nothing. Pretty soon his hat came flying out my office door, and he scrambled to grab it before it got run over by a passing garbage truck.

I couldn't resist nodding to him and giving him a sardonic smile as I opened the door and went inside.

Agnes was at her usual place behind her desk, looking as if she just ate a canary, feathers and all, and Wide Track Wilkie was standing in the center of the storefront window, fists on his hips, watching Bardot go.

"Hey, Wide."

"Herm." He nodded absently.

"I see you've met our friendly wannabe bonding tycoon."

"Asshole had the nerve to tell me to fuck off and mind my own business. You believe that?"

"Shocking," I said. "Also very disrespectful."

"Yeah, that's what I said, too. Didn't I say that, Miss Agnes?"

"Well," said Agnes, "not exactly. I seem to recall your words were a bit shorter than that."

"Yeah, whatever. Anyways, I had to slam him into the wall a couple times, just to see how good he bounced."

"And did he?"

"Not worth a shit."

"So you told him to have a nice day and invited him to leave?"

"Just like that."

Agnes snorted. Now they were both grinning.

"How about your research?" I said. "Do we know anything more about him?"

He lost the grin, wrinkled his brow and shook his head. "Not much. The word on the street is he's some kind of outcast from the Chicago mob, but he's got no record under the name he's using right now. Maybe this will help." He reached in the pocket of his trench coat and pulled out a well-worn leather wallet.

"This is his?" I said.

"Not anymore."

Agnes chuckled and shook her head in mock disapproval.

"Does he know you've got it?"

"Not yet."

"Better and better. Let's just see what we can see here. Then we'll copy what we need and throw the wallet out on the sidewalk for him to come back and find later."

"I'm not leaving any money in it."

I pulled out maybe two or three hundred in small bills and gave it to him. Then I pulled out three different drivers' licenses in three names, some credit cards that matched each of them, and one of those little envelopes that you get at hotels, to hold your key and tell you what your room number is. I handled them all by the edges. I took them over to my copy machine, copied both sides of everything, and put it all back together.

"Does the wallet itself have your prints on it?" I said to Wilkie.

"It would have to, yeah."

"I meant on the inside."

"No. I didn't open it."

I took a tissue from a dispenser on Agnes' desk and wiped down the entire outside of the wallet. Then I threw it in a drawer of my own desk and locked it.

"What happened to leaving it on the sidewalk?"

"I just got a better idea."

"Which is?"

"You're better off not knowing. What about the other thing, the fingerprints from the snow shovel?"

"That's another big awshit. We lifted some okay prints, but they're not in the criminal info computer."

"You still have them?"

"Sort of. I've got a CD that describes them to a computer. Or I think that's what it does."

"That's even better. Do you happen to know if The Prophet is still in business at his old digs?"

"The crazy guy? As far as I know."

"He's not crazy, he just marches to the beat of a different kazoo."

"He talks to people who aren't there, Herm. And I mean without using a phone."

"Well, there is that, yes. But he also talks to just about any secure data base you can think of."

"And we need that?" His face told me he was hoping for a no.

"We need it, Wide. I'm thinking our fingerprint might be in a military or government file. But you don't have to come along, if you really can't stand the guy."

"Well, I'm already in the game, you know?" He sighed. "I'll see the next card."

I told Agnes that if Anne Packard called, she should give her Wilkie's cell phone number. Then he and I headed for the door.

"Have a nice day, Miss Agnes."

"Why, thank you, Wendell. You, too."

<><><>

He insisted that his only name was The Prophet, so that's what we always called him to his face. To ourselves, we mostly called him the Proph. In the summers, he lived in a junker of a step van that was permanently parked in the alley behind a defunct furniture store. He spent his days misquoting scripture and dispensing pearls of incomprehensible wisdom to anybody who would listen. But when the weather turned cold, he moved back into an old two-story brick building on the far East Side, next to some railroad tracks. I think it used to be a switch house or some other kind of railroad maintenance building, back when there were lots more tracks and the BN&SF was the Soo Line or even earlier, when it was the Great Northern or the Union Pacific.

Whatever railroad it was, it lost interest in the building a long time ago but didn't bother to wreck it, and The Prophet had been squatting there for several years. He stole power from a nearby transformer that didn't get looked at much and phone service from who knows where, and he supported himself and his ersatz ministry by engaging in some of the most effective hacking known to nerd-dom. I had used his services before.

Like his van, the building was painted with a lot of strange proclamations, like crude, oversized bumper stickers. "Yah! Is my god!" done in six-foot-high shadow lettering and four colors was the most prominent. Off to the sides were slogans that hadn't been rendered quite so elaborately. "THE LIVING ARE NOT NEARLY SO ALIVE AS THE DEAD ARE DEAD," was one. Another said, "He that diggeth a pit shall fall in it," and a partially painted-over one said something about "A Land Flowing With Bilk and Money." The over-painting said, "The meek shall inherit the earth, complete with windfall profit, state, dog, and syn taxes."

There was a door on the side of the building facing the tracks. Wilkie pulled it open, and we found ourselves looking into a small black closet with a full-length mirror facing us. We stood there a while, looking at ourselves looking stupid, and then the ceiling spoke.

"Praise Yah!" it said, in a tinny voice.

"Yeah?" I said.

"You pronounce it wrong," said the ceiling. I smiled, because we had had this exact conversation before.

"There's a lot of that going around," I said.

"Pilgrim? Is that you?"

"In the willing flesh. Wilkie's with me."

"Praise Yah, already," said Wilkie, looking disgusted. He knows that I'm the only one who gets to go inside without saying that.

"Make it!" said the ceiling.

There was a loud buzzing noise, and one of the walls of the closet turned into a door that popped open. We went through it, bumbled around two more corners, and finally emerged into the main building. Most of the windowless room was taken up by a huge workbench covered with multiple-screen computers, printers, and a dozen other gizmos that I couldn't identify. Tangles of wire were everywhere, as were little plastic boxes that had colored lights blinking in no identifiable pattern. Behind it all, in a rattan peacock chair, sat a small, wizened black man with a full beard and a Nike headband. He smiled broadly at us.

"Welcome to my inner sanctum," he said. "You have been a long time wandering in the wilderness, Pilgrim."

"Well, there's a lot of it out there."

"Disheartening, is it not?"

"What's with the new door setup?" said Wilkie.

"You like that?"

"No."

"It repels bad joss." He continued to smile as if Wilkie hadn't spoken. "Good joss meanders and insinuates and can always get in, but bad joss travels in straight lines and gets reflected back by the mirror. Also, it can't get around all the corners."

"Told you," I said.

"You never."

"Yah told me you would come," said The Prophet.

"Well, he always does, doesn't he?" I said.

"I bet he doesn't say when, though, does he?" said Wilkie.

"He said you would be seeking enlightenment. Have I told you how the world tripped into the beginning of its present utter, irreversible madness in 1955, when people wanted coffee tables and picture windows?"

"Yes," I said.

"Really? How was it?"

"Long."

He frowned a bit and pursed his lips. "Hmm. Maybe I did tell you. What is it you seek today?"

"Is information the same as enlightenment?" said Wilkie.

"No," said The Prophet. "Enlightenment, if you can find it, is free. Information costs. If it's illegal, five hundred, minimum."

"Steep," said Wilkie.

"But worthy of it," said the Prophet.

"'A good name is rather to be chosen than great riches,'" I said.

"Very good, Pilgrim. Proverbs, Chapter 22. But Ecclesiastes says, 'Wine maketh merry, but money answerith all things.' Five cee won't ruin my good name or your profit-and-loss sheet."

If he only knew.

"'A word fitly spoken is like apples of gold in pictures of silver,'" I said. You have to do a lot of homework to dicker with The Prophet.

"Could be," he said. "Have you got one?"

"Sure. 'The race is not to the swift, nor the battle to the strong, but that's the way the smart money bets.'"

He looked at me for a while with some surprise on his face. Finally, he broke out into a smile.

"That's not bad," he said. "I can use that. All right, for the sake of your golden words, two-fifty, but it could go up if the stuff gets tricky."

"Fair enough."

I laid five fifties on his desk, and we got down to business. "Army personnel records," I said. "Vietnam era."

He began massaging two separate keyboards with great concentration, shutting out anything else we might say for a while. I noticed that although his chair was straight off the set of some Tennessee Williams play, it was nevertheless fitted with swivel castors, and he had a good time whizzing around on them, sometimes for no apparent reason. Finally he stopped and asked me for some more specific direction.

"I need the roster of a company that was in-country in about 1965. Echo Company, with the First Air Cavalry."

"Brigade and Battalion, Pilgrim."

"Excuse me?"

"The First Air Cav would be a division. It splits into brigades, then battalions, and then finally companies. That's a lot of damn heathens."

"You seem to know an awful lot about army organization, for a holy man."

"When the walls of Jericho came tumbling down, I said *Kaddish* for the people buried under the rubble. I was a chaplain in the Fifth Roman Legion at the time. When the—"

"You've also got an organization chart on the screen in front of you," said Wilkie.

"To download is to know, oh great one."

Wilkie snorted. The Prophet continued to work mouse and keyboard. Sometimes I wished he weren't so useful, so I could tell him how full of shit I thought he was.

"So a division is how many souls?" I said.

"Ten or fifteen thousand, with bodies attached."

"That could cost fifty bucks just for the paper to print it out," said Wilkie. I could stand for him to be a lot less helpful at times.

"Let's attack it from the other end," I said. "Find the record of Charles Victor, and see what unit he was in, back then." I gave him Charlie's service number, which I had pulled from one of his bond files.

"Which year, Pilgrim?"

"Work that backward, too, if you can. Go for a time when he was a newly minted corporal."

He fired up a second screen and did a lot of looking back and forth between the two of them.

"July, 1966. Looks like the company had three platoons, about twenty people per. You want all of them?"

"What I really want is the last known address of each of them."

"You're a hard taskmaster."

"Remember the golden apples."

"Hmm. I'll write a short program to pull them up. Perhaps you would like a cup of my famous tea while you wait?"

"Is it hallucinogenic?"

"Only a little. It will not affect your ability to drive, I think."

"Um. Got any coffee?"

"Timid souls. There's instant over by the sink, hot water in the carafe." Wilkie and I helped ourselves, and the Prophet got back to work. After a while, he punched a last key, and machines began to click and whirr on their own. Now and then, a list of names would come out of the printer.

"Anything else, while we're waiting for that to finish?"

Wilkie reached into an inside pocket a pulled out the CD in its plastic envelope.

"Fingerprint," he said. "Put into some kind of electronic code, I guess. It's not a picture anymore, anyway."

"And you want me to check it for a criminal record?"

"Nah, we already tried that and came up dry. We were thinking maybe it would be in the Army's records."

"Ah." He took the disc and fed it into yet another machine. Almost too fast to be believable, he said, "It's there, all right."

"And?"

"Classified."

"How the hell can a Fingerprint be classified?" said Wilkie. "I mean, aren't all these files we're looking at classified? Why can't we look at it anyway?"

"This is classified the way the true name of Buddha is classified, big man. I mean, *nobody* has the key to this."

"Black ops?" I said.

"Could be. That, or the man simply had a friend in records and put the lock on it himself. Some sojourners prefer to go about anonymously."

"Isn't that the truth, though?"

"Anything else?"

"One thing," I said. "While your machine is still back in 1966, see which brigade Charlie was in."

"Easy. Q.E.D."

"Why brigade?" said Wilkie.

"Because I think that's the highest level that still has a commanding officer who is actually in the field, with the troops." And therefore could have been assassinated in the field. Also because I had a hunch, but I wasn't sure enough of it to say so just yet.

"Got it," said the Prophet.

"Now see who commands that same outfit today."

That took a little longer, but he got that, too.

"The name of the soul is Rappolt."

"No way," I said. "I'm sorry to be the one to tell you, Prophet, but you screwed up. You're still back in the sixties, and Rappolt was a lieutenant."

"Not so. Look for yourself. Colonel John S. Rappolt, the Third. He took command less than a year ago."

"Well, I'll be go to hell."

"Not in my inner sanctum, you won't."

"What's the big deal?" said Wilkie.

"We're not looking for a service buddy, after all," I said, "we're looking for kin. John Rappolt was the name of the first officer Charlie ever fragged."

"Not that common a name," said Wilkie.

"It sure isn't. I'm thinking this is his son."

"Could be a grandson, by now."

"I don't think so. Not an immediate enough link. I'm thinking it's somebody who grew up fatherless on account of Charlie and has been pissed off about it ever since. Somebody who took a long time and went to a lot of trouble to find out who to kill. Can you get me a picture of him, Prophet?"

"Coming out of the printer now."

It was a face I had never seen before.

"Wide, you were in the Army, weren't you?"

"Don't remind me. Yeah, I was in Desert Storm."

"So tell me: if a colonel decided to go off duty and off the radar to kill somebody, who would he trust to go with him?"

"That's easy. He'd take his sergeant major."

"Isn't that two people?"

"It's a hybrid rank," he said, shaking his head. "It's the battalion commander's link to the grunts, and the two of them are usually tighter than cell mates."

"And what about the others?"

"A sergeant major would have a few enlisteds who are more loyal to him personally then they are to the army. It wouldn't be hard to find a few to go along. In the current crop of grunts, there would even be some who would make the trip just for the chance to break some rules and raise a little hell."

"Who pays for this supposed operation?"

"Rappolt, of course. He's a full colonel, Herm. He's got money coming out of his brass ears."

"That much?"

"Hey, it's an officers' corps. Always was, always will be."

I looked back at the Prophet and said, "Can we find Rappolt's sergeant major?"

Two minutes later, we had the name of a Sergeant Major Robert Dunne.

"You want a picture of him, too?"

"Yes."

His picture shouldn't have surprised me, but it did. A line at a time, the machine spat out the face of a fiftyish man in full dress uniform. He'd worn a uniform the last time I saw him, too, but not that one. It was the beefy-faced cop that I had followed into Nighttown.

"Do you have a fax?" I said.

"Is the Pope a child molester?" He spread his palms outward and grinned.

"I take that for a yes. I'll need a regular phone, too."

"Secure?"

"It doesn't matter."

"Then I don't have one."

"All right, then, secure."

"Twenty bucks, Pilgrim."

"You're something else, you know that?"

"I am the thing nobody knows how to cope with: a genuine holy man with business sense."

"Wide, loan me your phone, okay?"

"Some people just don't believe in free trade." The Proph went off somewhere to sulk.

I called Anne at work and got her fax number, so I could send her all the stuff we had just printed. But she had something else on her mind, as well.

"I'm glad you called," she said. "I think I know where your dead man's tunnel is."

The Road to the Jungle

Anne had found out about the tunnel quite by accident, chatting with an old-time staffer at her newspaper about the problems of interacting with the pressmen, who were across the river and a mile away. Email was all well and good, he said, but it was better when the presses were just down the street, at Fourth and Minnesota.

"They were? How did they get the big rolls of paper there?" she had idly asked. "Don't they always come in by rail? There are no train tracks on Fourth Street, never were."

The answer was that there was a long, sloping tunnel that ran down from the basement of the old press building, south, under Kellogg Boulevard, under Kellogg Park (né Viaduct Park,) and finally down to a small warehouse by the railroad tracks. The tunnel daylighted on the Mississippi river flats, at the base of the limestone bluffs that hold up Downtown. When the press building was wrecked and replaced with a parking ramp, the little warehouse down by the tracks was also leveled, and the tunnel was simply sealed up and abandoned.

I let Wilkie and The Prophet listen in on my phone call with Anne. It turned out that The Prophet also knew where Charlie's tunnel was. Silly soul that I am, I had neglected to ask him. He knew most of what went on in the homeless community, but he never volunteered anything that wasn't either for enlightenment or for sale.

"That place is full of bad joss, Pilgrim. Maybe demons, too. And it's all linear, so you can't dodge them. Nobody ever followed your man Cee Vee in there. Nobody even talks about what's in there."

"Where is the entrance, exactly?"

"Trust me, you do not want to go there."

"I have to."

"Then may Yah! protect you."

"Where?"

He told me.

⟨⟩⟨⟩⟨⟩

I had promised Anne that I wouldn't go in the tunnel until she could get clear of her office and maybe bring a photographer with her. That would be about two hours, she said. Tight, but doable, if everything went right.

I drove back downtown from The Prophet's place and dropped Wilkie off at Lefty's. He didn't like the idea of being cut out of the action, but I told him I had to do some things that were better done without any witnesses. That, he could dig. I went to my office and took a few things out of my desk, including the copy of Charlie's Master key and Eddie Bardot's wallet. Then I took my copy of Charlie's will, penned a quick note to myself and headed out.

"Leaving again so soon?" said Agnes.

"Got to. Can't let the bad joss catch up with me."

"Well, I definitely know who you've been talking to. Where will you be, if anybody asks?"

"If anybody asks, you think I went to Lefty's."

"And if I ask?"

"I'm off to play tunnel rat. I also need you to make a couple of phone calls for me, but not just yet."

"Honestly, Herman, why don't you just give up and get a cell—"

"Don't even start, Agnes."

⟨⟩⟨⟩⟨⟩

The rail yard that used to cover the river flats below Downtown is almost all gone now, mostly ripped out and replaced with contract-only parking lots. That makes the base of the bluff not so easy to get to anymore. I parked a quarter of a mile to the west, near the sally port entrance to the County Jail, took a flashlight out of my trunk, and walked back east, under the Wabasha Bridge. I followed the limestone rubble at the bottom of the looming wall of stone, skirting the parking lots that were baking in the late afternoon sun.

There were a lot of openings in the bluff face that had been plugged up with concrete or bricks. Most of them were quite high up, including a lot of them right under the steeply sloping roadway of Second Street. But down at base level, almost blocked by fallen stones and sand, was one that had not been simply bricked in. It had a rusty steel door built into the brickwork, with a hasp and a padlock. I took the copy of Charlie's key out of my pocket and tried it.

Click.

I swung the door toward myself, and it drew with it a breath of musty, cold air. It smelled like wet limestone and dead rats and failed dreams. It smelled like fear. I pulled the door open as far as it would go, clicked on the flashlight and walked into Charlie Victor's nightmares.

The machinery for moving the big rolls of paper was still there, sort of a trough-shaped skeletal steel framework with rollers on the cross-frames and a heavy chain running down the center. The chain had big hooks on it at regular intervals, and it looked like something out of a mechanized slaughterhouse for elephants.

The rusted conveyor took up most of the tunnel width, but there was room enough to walk alongside it on the left. Service access, probably. I imagined that once in a while a roll of paper would fall off the frame or get stuck, and some poor bastards would have to go into the tunnel and fix it. I also imagined that they didn't like the job much. I wasn't quite ready to start using terms like "bad joss," but the place did not have a good feel to it. I found myself walking with my shoulders hunched. Whether you think you're claustrophobic or not, the thought of about a million tons of earth above your head is going to be oppressive. There also seemed to be a draft at my back, which didn't help my mood any.

I had left the door fully open, but a dozen steps into the tunnel, it provided no light at all. I turned around now and then to satisfy myself that it was still there, an increasingly small white rectangle in a universe of black. Not an auspicious thing, having the light at the end of the tunnel behind your back.

My flashlight was woefully inadequate, and I used the steel framework like a banister, to keep myself oriented and to pull myself up at times. The tunnel floor was a soft, yellowish sand, almost a powder, and it sloped upward fairly steeply. Walking up it was a lot of work. Now and then something would drip onto my face and arms, cold and startling. If it was something other than just water, I didn't want to think about it. And then there was the other thing.

I didn't call it a ghost, and I didn't think it was the Prophet's demons, either, but there was definitely some kind of *presence* in the tunnel. And somehow or other, it was both with me and waiting for me to arrive. Was the Prophet's instant coffee hallucinogenic, as well as his tea? Would he have told me if it was? I let my guts feel what they wanted to and forced my feet to move forward in spite of it. I had a job to do. I did not have to be comfortable doing it.

After maybe fifty or sixty yards, I came to a smaller tunnel, crossing the main one, with some kind of pipe in it. I tried shining my flashlight down it to see if it looked worth exploring, then shone it on the floor to see if there were any obvious footprints going into it. That's when I saw the first of the white powder.

It crossed the path of the pipe and made a sort of one-pronged arrow, pointing deeper into the main passage. What was it Charlie had told me about marking his path in the VC tunnels?

I never used string, Harold. Somebody can move string on you. Some kind of white powder is better, some flour or baking powder, or something. You got to put it off to one side, so you don't accidentally scuff it out, but it never moves on you. And the enemy don't have any of the stuff.

It wasn't a lot lighter in color than the sand of the floor, but now that I knew what to look for, I spotted lots more of it, always directing me farther up the main tunnel.

I passed another small pipe tunnel, then a bigger cross-passage that looked natural, rather than man-made. It looked irregular and deep, and the draft I had felt at my back seemed to be flowing into it. And there was a string on its floor, leading straight away from me and into the darkness. I smiled and continued the way I had been going. I imagined hearing Charlie chuckle and say *I knew you'd be too smart for that one, Herbert.*

I must have been under Kellogg Boulevard by then, deep underground, where the temperature should have been a constant fifty degrees or so. It felt colder. I remembered Charlie telling me it got too cold in his box for him to stay there all winter, and I wondered if he was confusing the chill in the tunnel with the chill in his soul. This was a place where you could have a lot of chill in your soul.

I was starting to get short of breath from the climb and was about to stop for a bit when I came to another side-tunnel, this time with a definite white arrow pointing into it. I turned into it, sorry to leave the reassuring touch of the steel rail. I was swimming in thick blackness now. I moved forward a bit more slowly, sweeping the flashlight around a lot, pushing one hand out in front of me to grope at nothing. Somewhere up ahead, I could hear the faint gurgle of rushing water. Storm sewer, probably. Not a good thing to walk into.

The passage ended in a great black hole, which I assumed dropped to a main storm sewer line somewhere far below. But before that, there was a slightly wider spot in the floor and a messy campsite. I was there.

As promised so long ago, there was a cardboard box big enough for a person to sleep in, "under the wye-duct." It had a tattered sleeping bag, some clothes, and a few rags in it. They smelled like mildew. In front of the box was a small Coleman camp stove, some assorted full and empty tin cans, a green glass wine jug, and other junk not so easy to identify. Several candles sat in various kinds of holders with wax dribbled all over them. And behind it all, in a niche in the wall, was a box, a heavy white cardboard box of the sort that offices use to archive their paper files. But this one, I positively knew, contained something else. I had found Charlie Victor's frag box.

I lifted the lid and found Addendum Number One to Charlie's last will and testament, sitting on top of a big pile of cash.

Then I heard the noise.

Fire in the Hole

It came from far behind me, echoing back up the unseen rock walls. It wasn't a boom, exactly, but it wasn't a machine noise, either. I went back to the place where my tunnel joined the bigger one, killed the flashlight and looked around the corner. The light at the end of the tunnel, the door opening, tiny as it had been, was gone. What I had heard was somebody slamming the door.

I could hear voices now, too, but not well enough to make out what they were saying. Fairly young voices, male, wise cracking but insistent. The goon squad from the scene at the motel, and this time I had no shotgun to point at them.

And why had they shut the door? *Because they have night vision goggles, and they know you don't, dummy.* Shit.

I ran back to Charlie's squat and put the lid back on his box. Then, as fast as I could, I dug a hole in the soft sand floor with my hands, shoved the box in it, and pulled Charlie's big sleeping-box over the top. Then I scuffled the area where I had dragged it and got the hell out of there. I didn't know what my plan was, but being found at the campsite seemed like a very bad idea.

I went back to the main tunnel, killed my flashlight again, and groped my way across to the steel conveyor frame. As quickly as I could in the dark, I worked my way down into the lower framework and against the back wall. Then I crawled uphill maybe another dozen yards or so, banging various parts of my anatomy on the steel, and finally stuffed myself into a hollow in the limestone wall. I pushed some loose sand into a heap in front of me and settled down to wait. It wasn't much of a hiding place, but it was as good as I could do. I had to count on people not looking too closely into the jumble of angle irons and chains. And if they all went into the campsite cavern, maybe I could slip past them and work my way back outside. Maybe. It would have to do.

The voices began to get louder. I pulled my jacket up over my head, to hide my face and eyes, and worked on quieting my breathing.

Bring back memories, does it?

What?

Detroit, boyo.

Who the hell…?

What, has it been so long that you've forgotten the sound of me lilting voice already?

Jerp?

Himself. How've you been, lad?

This is crazy; you're dead.

Picked right up on that, did you? Of course I'm dead. I couldn't very well be here if I wasn't, now could I?

You're not. You came out of a cup of the Prophet's doped coffee. You're nothing but a piece of abnormal brain chemistry.

I've been called worse, I suppose.

No kidding. Since you're here, though, I'll tell you that I'm sorry I abandoned you in Detroit. I mean, I didn't want to, but you said—

Hush it now, then. I bled to death behind the wheel of the Mercury, is the thing. That's what I did. I didn't burn up. But if we'd ha' gone straight to the hospital, I'd bled to death before we got there, too. The thing of it is, I forgave you before I even drew me last breath. Time you forgave yourself, you hear?

I hear.

It's time and a half, and that's the truth of it. Can you do it?

I have to say, I needed to hear that, Jerp. But yes, I can do it. Two days ago, I'd have said no, but I had a sort of awakening, in an alley up on the Iron Range.

An awakening?

Call it a sea change.

Ah, one of them.

Now it's not only possible, it's easy.

That's the stuff, then.

Thanks.

Don't give it a thought, lad. So how are you getting on here, then?

Here? Not so well.

Not about to join me, are you?

No. I'll die soon enough, like anybody else, but not today and not here. I don't know what I'm going to do, exactly, but I know that much.

Now you're talking, lad.

He sure is.

And just who the hell is this, then?

Jesus, I don't believe this. It's a regular party. That's Charlie. You two have a lot in common; he's dead, too.

I may be dead, Humboldt, but I ain't gone. You want I should take care of those goons for you?

I don't think you can scare them, away, Charlie.

Oh, I can do lots better than that. Sit tight; I think you'll like this.

Sit tight, he says.

You wouldn't happen to have a drop of the pure, in a hip flask or some such, now, would you?

You can't drink; you're dead.

I meant for yourself.

Losing my mind is bad enough, Jerp. I don't think I'll add getting drunk.

Suit yourself, lad.

Far down the tunnel, voices that were altogether too real replaced the ones in my head.

"Hey, there's a string going down this one."

"So?"

"So, I bet it's a trail marker."

"Could be. Or it could be a string. Dipshit. Are there any tracks?"

"Hell, this whole place is nothing but tracks. And in the soft sand, you can't tell the old ones from our own."

"What's that smell? Sort of like—"

"Hey, I saw the string jerk!"

"Jesus, me, too! Run it down fast, before our man has a chance to pull it all in!"

"You want me to stay and keep watch in the main tunnel?"

"What for? We know where he is now. Let's move it!"

There were a lot of scuffling noises and some clatter of gear. It and the voices gradually got more muted, until I couldn't make out the words any more, even though they were shouting now. Then for a short while, everything was silent.

And then there was the loudest explosion I have ever heard, accompanied by a flashbulb illumination of the whole place. After half a second or so, there was another, and then a third. Charlie's string had led straight to a whole cluster of booby traps.

Soft dust rained down on me, and for a long time the whole tunnel seemed to ring like a piece of steel on an anvil.

After a while, when I heard nothing more, I went back to Charlie's campsite and made the appropriate adjustments to the box, then put it back where I had first found it. Then I walked back out. The door at the bottom of the tunnel had blown back open, and the draft that I had felt when I first walked in was blowing smoke and dust into the side passage where the explosion had been. I stopped and watched it swirl in the beam of my flashlight for a while, thinking it was beautiful. It looked like deliverance.

Then I was outside, squinting into the daylight. Looking at my watch, I saw that less than an hour had passed since I had first opened Charlie's padlock. Amazing stuff, time. I still had enough of it to brush the dust off myself and maybe get my hearing back to normal. If my hands stopped shaking, that would be nice, too.

I did not hear any more voices from the tunnel, either of soldiers or ghosts.

Shots in the Dark

Anne showed up an hour or so later, just as promised, with a staff photographer, a sort of angular young woman named Chris. She wore jeans and a lumberjack shirt and vest and had a brown ponytail poking out of the back of a baseball cap. She made me think of the skipper of a swordfish boat.

"Anne tells me good things about you," she said as she shook my hand.

"How nice of her. Maybe some time you'll share them with me."

"Maybe not," said Anne. Then she looked at the still-open door to the cavern and gave me an arched eyebrow and a very hard look.

"You said you were going to wait for us, Herman. If the scene isn't original, I can't——"

"I think somebody else got here ahead of us," I said. It wasn't *quite* a lie, but it wasn't really an answer, either.

"You think it's safe to go in?"

"If we're careful. There was an explosion about an hour ago, and nobody has come out since then. I think somebody walked into one of Charlie's booby traps."

"Maybe we should wait for some police or fire people. The Bomb Squad. Chris, do you want a vote?"

"You know me, Anne. If there's a picture in there, I'm going. And if the authorities go in ahead of us, they'll shut us out, for sure." She started fooling with some of the gear that she carried in her vest, which seemed to be all pockets.

"Then we're off," said Anne.

"Just a little," I said, "and it hardly shows."

"Video cam for openers, I think," said Chris. "Mr. Jackson, it would be best if you went first, so there's someone in the picture for scale. Here's an extra battle lantern for you."

She handed me the biggest flashlight I have ever seen, and we set off to find the Wizard.

<><><>

I was just as glad the others were behind my back, since I couldn't tell how good a job I was doing of pretending I hadn't been there before. When we came to the branch cavern that had smoke and dust still drifting back into it, I explained to them about the string and the white powder.

"Let the Bomb Squad go down that passage," I said. "Later, though. Charlie wanted us to go the other way."

And when we finally came to Charlie's squat, I managed to be as surprised and delighted as everybody else. Chris switched to a digital SLR with a big flash and photographed me pointing at the frag box, then checking the lid for wires or other trip devices, and finally opening it and holding up the hand-written note that was on top of the money, then some of the money itself.

"Do we dare take it outside?" said Chris. "I mean, it could be like a crime scene or something."

"I'll worry about that, if you don't mind." Agent Krause, right on cue.

"Would you identify yourself, for the record?" said Chris, switching back to her video camera and swinging it around.

"I am Special Agent Krause, of the United States Secret Service."

"Nice to meet you. We are—"

"You are the person who is shutting off her camera. This site and that box are evidence in an ongoing official investigation, and they are strictly classified. Shut it off now, unless you want to lose it."

"Nice to see you again, too," I said. "Where's your partner?"

"He's chasing what he foolishly thinks is a hot lead, down in Swede Hollow. Seems he had an anonymous phone call." She went over to the box and peered inside it.

"But you came here instead?" said Anne.

"Apparently my anonymous phone calls are better than his." Good old Agnes.

Kraus pulled out the note and read it in the light of her own flashlight. She smirked. Seeing her do so, I stifled the urge to follow suit.

"Good stuff, Agent?"

"None of your business, Jackson. Tell you what, though: you can carry it outside for me. We're leaving this place, people. Now. You over there, is your camera off?"

Chris pointed it at her and said, "The little red light is off. See?"

I thought the little red light looked as if it had a piece of black electrical tape over it, but I saw no reason to tell Krause that.

"Let's go," said Krause.

And we did. I led the parade back to the real world, carrying the frag box, with Agent Smug close behind and Chris and Anne bringing up the rear. About halfway back, there was another problem with the light at the end of the tunnel. It didn't get shut this time, but somebody stepped in front of it. I recognized the silhouette of the man I now knew to be Sergeant Major Robert Dunne. He had his phony cop uniform on again, and both it and he were looking burnt and bloodied.

You think you used enough explosive, Charlie?

There didn't seem to be anything wrong with the submachine gun Dunne was holding, though.

There was no way I could jump out of his field of fire, so I did what I hoped was the next best thing: I shone my light in his face and tried to close the distance between us. I didn't get very far.

"Point that light someplace else, or I'll blow you and it both to hell."

I pointed the light at the floor. Behind me, Krause did the same. But she, too, was moving up.

"I thought I told you to shut your operation down and get out of town," said Krause.

"As a matter of fact, Agent, you did not. In your typical arrogant manner, you ordered us to take our operation out of the public eye, quote-unquote. And I would say this is about as far out of it as we could get. I believe you're holding what I came here for, Jackson. Bring it here. Krause, you stay where you are."

"Where's the Colonel?" I said.

"Say again?"

"Colonel Rappolt, your boss."

"You know about him, do you? Impressive, for a dipshit civilian. But you obviously don't know much about the Army."

"How's that?"

"Colonels do not go on treasure hunting ops. And they do not do their own killing. He watched it, but he didn't get any licks in. He just spat on the guy afterward. And once the bum was dead, the colonel was done with it all. He didn't care about the box the guy told us about when we were beating on him. But I do. I just lost four good men looking for it. So give it up, now, and don't get cute."

"Me? I wouldn't think of it." I took a last step toward him and pretended to trip on a conveyor frame, dropping the box and falling on top of it. I was hoping to make a play for his gun, but Krause was too fast for me. The momentary distraction was all she needed to get her skinny automatic out of its secret hiding place and put about a dozen rounds into the sergeant major. Personally, I thought she was overreacting, but I can't honestly say I didn't approve.

I did wonder, though, if I would ever get my hearing back again.

Aftershock

When we got back out to the daylight, Anne called 911 before Krause could think to tell her not to. Soon we had a mob of police and fire people to contend with, including the Bomb Squad and a crime scene team. I even got to meet the elusive homicide cop, Detective Erickson, who turned out to be a fairly likeable guy. He and Krause were old buddies, it seemed, and he did nothing to stop her from leaving with Charlie's box. She also got to keep her weapon, and she confiscated the memory card from Chris' video cam.

"How can they do that?" said Chris.

"It's evidence in a conspiracy case," I said. "The Secret Service has had the power to seize that for as long as there has been a Secret Service."

"I bet we never see any of it again," she said.

"She promised I could have the money back, as soon as it's done being evidence," I said, "since I'm Charlie's legal heir."

"What will that be, a year or two?" said Anne.

"If ever," I said, thinking about the black hole that Krause had threatened to have me thrown into. Other things could be thrown into it, too. "And even if I get the money back, I'd bet the video and the note are permanently gone."

"Good thing nobody thought to take the memory card out of my SLR."

"Don't say that too loud," I said, "until we get clear of this place."

<><><>

Eventually we did get clear, finally running out of people who wanted to debrief and/or intimidate us. We all went down to Lefty's then, to do a bit of debriefing of our own. Anne stopped by her office on the way and got a laptop, and soon we were looking at an enlargement of the paper from Charlie's box. Chris had done a perfect job of shooting it. It was written on the back of a copy of Charlie's will, with some kind of fairly blunt felt-tip pen, printed all in caps.

DEAR HOBART

I ALWAYS KNEW YOU WOULD BE THE ONE WHO WOULD FIND THIS. THERE ISNT ENOUGH HERE TO BUY THE HIT ON THE PRESIDENT, BUT TAKE IT TO THIS GUY CALLS HIMSELF HOOK AND SEE WILL HE MAYBE DO IT ANYWAY CONSIDERING HOW THINGS WORKED OUT. YOULL FIND HIM AT THE ST. PAUL HOTEL UNDER THE NAME OF EDDIE BARDOT. HE MIGHT HAVE A COUPLA OTHER NAMES TOO. I COPPED SOME OF HIS CREDIT CARDS SO YOU CAN SEE THE OTHERS. THANKS FOR EVERYTHING

YOUR FRIEND CHARLIE VICTOR

"Who's Hobart?" said Chris.

"That's me," I said. "Charlie always called me something that started with H and had two syllables, but that's as close as he ever came to remembering my real name."

"How much money was there in the box?"

"I didn't have time to count it, but I thought it looked like about five thousand."

"And who's this Bardot person?"

"Who knows?" I shrugged. "Maybe a real assassin, maybe just a con artist. Krause won't care."

"So that's it, then," said Anne. "Agent Krause gets her big bust—"

"She could use one," said Chris.

"Oh, nasty," I said. "Correct, but nasty."

"She gets her big *collar*," said Anne, "and the guys who killed Charlie are all dead."

"Except for Rappolt," I said.

"Oh, yes. Him. Did you mention him to the police?"

"No. I figured there was no point. He's back in wherever he's officially supposed to be by now, with a ton of plausible deniability in front of him. And no way the Army investigates a full colonel on the say so of a mere civilian."

"You're probably right. I don't have enough hard data to use him in my write-up, so how much less is anybody in authority going to pursue it? Oh, well."

"I trust it's a usable story anyway?"

"Oh, it's a hell of a story, Herman."

<>‹›<>

Anne's story ran two days later. The Secret Service, of course, pressured her editor about the need for secrecy in the assassination case, and he partially agreed. She was not allowed to say anything about the hit man named in the note, nor about any hit man, period. She was allowed to tell about the tunnel and the box, but only as a secret stash of money from unknown sources.

But that was enough. She wrote a very solid piece about Charlie's and his father's murders and their connection to the Vietnam War. It had sensational crime reporting, human interest, history, and just a hint of conspiracy, and it ran on the front page. She also did a sidebar on the lives of homeless people, with a picture of Glenda. That ran in an interior section of the same issue. She wanted to do another one on the abuses of power by the Department of Homeland Security, if only to get back at Agent Krause for stealing her video, but her editor wouldn't buy it.

We celebrated the printing by going out to dinner at a sports bar that superficially resembled the dance hall in Eveleth. They didn't have a band, though. For dancing and other activity, we had to go back to my townhouse. Later, we sat on the big couch in front of the fireplace, watching the gas log pretend to burn itself up and working on a bottle of my best Scotch.

"Seems like it was a long way for you to go, just for a story in one issue of the newspaper," I said.

"Sometimes it happens that way."

"Was it worth it?"

"False modesty does not become you, Jackson. What you mean is were *you* worth it. I shouldn't have to tell you so, but yes. But the story? Of course it was. There's always a bit of a letdown after a big story, though. It feels as if you never really quite knew as much as you would have liked before you wrote it."

"Maybe you'd have written it the same way anyway."

"Maybe. I'll never know. The thing about Rappolt bothers me."

"You mean that you couldn't include him in the piece?"

"No, that he gets off scot-free and nobody can do a thing about it. Doesn't that bother you?"

"Actually, he didn't quite get off. I had my hacker friend send an email to him, with a cc to his superior, telling him that his operation is blown and all his people dead."

"So, what will happen?"

"I don't know. His hometown is Kansas City. I thought I'd watch the local newspaper for a while at the Central Library, see if there's anything about him."

"You can do that online, you know."

"You can do a lot of things online, Anne, but that doesn't necessarily make them any better. I like tactile events. I like touching something besides a mouse."

"I noticed." She gave me a sly smile.

"Is that a complaint?"

"Not on your life."

"Anyway, whatever happens with Rappolt, Charlie wouldn't have cared, one way or the other."

"How can you be so sure of that?"

I let out a huge sigh, took my arm back from where it had been wrapped around her shoulders, and stood up. I had just made a very risky decision, one that was most unlike me.

"I'm about to give you a gift, Anne. It's a hell of a gift, and I'm betting a lot on your not taking advantage of it."

"You're talking like a soap opera, Herman. What are you giving me that is so precious?"

"The truth."

I went to my desk in the corner of the dining room, unlocked the center drawer, and took out a stained and crumpled sheet of paper. As I handed it to her, I said, "This is what was really on top of the money in Charlie's box."

"What was *really* there? But how could you have changed it? I mean, I saw you pick the other one up."

"A lot of things are possible in a dark tunnel, Anne. Did you wonder at all why Charlie would have written the note on the back of a copy of his will?"

"I guess I didn't think about it. Maybe that was the only paper he had."

"Wrong. It was the only paper *I* had with *his* fingerprints on it. So that's what I had to use for the forgery. This, however, is the McCoy."

She put down her glass of Scotch and read:

Dear Hubert,

I figured you would find this if anybody could. That's why I wrote that will. Once, I would have told you to take the money and use it to kill some people. A whole list of them. But I finally lived long enough to learn some things. I learned that blood feuds are no damn good. And I learned that the way that you stop them is just to stop.

I'm sick of the killing and the planning to kill and the hate. I want it to end with me. So take the money and do something good with it, okay? Maybe you can buy a bond for some homeless person.

That's a joke.

Thanks for all your help over the years. I'm proud to have known you.

Your dead friend,

Charlie

‹›‹›‹›

"You're right," she said. "He wouldn't have cared about Rappolt. In fact, it sounds as if he knew about him and still didn't care."

"And by not caring, he may have finally found his way out of the jungle."

"That's nice, Herman. I wish I could write it. What are you going to do with the money, assuming you ever get it back?"

"Actually, I didn't wait. I gave a free bond to a guy named Vitrol Wilson, who is a guaranteed skip. The question is what are you going to do with that piece of paper?"

She looked at it again. Then she got up, walked across the room, and threw it into the fire.

"Would you like to dance, Herman?"

"I'd love to."

‹›‹›‹›

The next day we held a memorial service for Charlie, down in Connemara Gulch. As his only heir, I had donated his remains to the med school at the University of Minnesota, but we solemnly buried his fatigue jacket and dog tags in a place by some small trees and marked the spot with a cross of baking powder. It took a while for the word to spread, but we eventually drew about twenty raggedy people for the event.

I had brought six bottles of wine with screw tops and a huge bag of White Castle hamburgers, but nobody was allowed to have anything without first standing over the grave and saying a few words. Some of them were actually quite moving. Apparently Charlie was well liked, even though he himself never admitted to liking anybody. The guy named Mingus, whose neck I had stood on only a few nights earlier, produced a harmonica and played "Amazing Grace" while each of the homeless people threw a handful of dirt into the hole and said "ashes to ashes," or something like that. One of them actually knew the Twenty-third Psalm, which he recited with some passion. One said, "Home is the soldier, home from the sea," and then got a look of major confusion and consternation. Another said, "There's a lot more of us laying down than there is up a-walking around." I shot him a quick glance to see if it might have been the Prophet.

Anne, true to her word, had brought a dozen copies of the newspaper with Glenda's picture in it. She gave them to her and showed her where to find the article.

As she looked at it, her eyes started to tear up.

"That ain't me! Why you printing somebody else's picture with my name? Dear, sweet suffering Jesus, I don't look like that!"

She looked again, squinting. "I don't, do I?"

"I'm sorry, Glenda. I thought you'd be happy to see—"

"Oh my God. I was never really beautiful, but I was at least… My God amighty. Where the hell have I got to?"

The tears were streaming freely down her face now, and soon her body was racked with sobs. Mingus put his harmonica back in his pocket and opened a bottle for her.

"Here you go, babe. Have a drink and forget about it."

She looked at the extended bottle for a long time, her crying subsiding a bit. Finally she said, "I don't think so."

"Sure, you do. It'll make everything okay. Don't it always?"

"I gotta go," was all she said, shaking her head vehemently. She gathered up her newspapers, clutched them to her bosom, and walked away.

I guessed it was a day for atonement and rebirth. I hoped so, anyway.

Epilogue

With Eddie Bardot snatched off the street, Wilkie was able to persuade Frank Russo to come back for his trial, after all. So the twenty-five thou I had taken out of Charlie's box, the first time I was in the tunnel, was pure gravy. I was back to playing with the house money. I gave Agnes her back pay and a week in advance for good measure. I didn't have the five K that the feds took, of course, but that was okay. They left town with Eddie in cuffs, just as happy as if they had good sense. He, presumably, was not so happy, and that was worth something to me.

Not long after that, there was an obituary in the *Kansas City Star* for a Colonel John Rappolt. Apparently he had done what a lot of self-important career officers do when they see their entire world fall apart. He had shot himself. So even though Charlie said he didn't care, I figured that all the shadows from his personal jungle were finally gone.

I wasn't sure if mine were, though, and I needed a detached, third party perspective to straighten out the issue. One morning, I headed north out of the Twin Cities, then crossed the St. Croix River into Wisconsin and went east on Highway Eight, across the recently harvested farmlands and into the brown and black late autumn countryside. I was going to a place that I visit seldom but think about often, all the way across Wisconsin and into Upper Michigan. Redrock Prison is its name, and it was where my uncle Fred was doing his fourth term for bookmaking.

After the usual pleasantries, I told him all about Charlie and his box and how I wasn't sure I had done enough truly to lay him to rest.

"Lemmie tell you a story, nephew," he said.

"Okay."

"Back about forty years ago, there was this guy, name of Eddie Feigner, was the fast-pitch king of softball. He could throw a softball, underhand, a hundred and twenty miles an hour, so fast the ref couldn't even see it. He was just the pure stuff, couldn't be beat.

"He was too good to play with any regular team, so he used to play traveling exhibition games, like the Harlem Globetrotters did in basketball. He traveled with just three other guys, a catcher and two fielders. They didn't need any basemen, see, 'cause Eddie would strike everybody out, but they had to have four men on the team so they had enough people to bat with the bases full. They called themselves 'The King and his Court.'"

"I seem to vaguely remember something about them."

"Yeah, I think I might have taken you to a game once when you were little. Okay, so anyway, here's our boy, at the end of the ninth inning in some nowhere little town. He's up by one run and there's two men out and he's got two strikes on the last batter. But he don't throw the ball. Instead, he's pacing around on the mound, looking worried. So the catcher goes out to talk to him.

"'Hey, man,' he says, 'we're one pitch away from winning this thing. Throw it, already.'

"'I gotta tell you,' Feigner says, 'I ain't got nothing left. My arm is shot. I'm not sure I can even get the ball to the plate, much less throw a strike. I think we gotta concede the game.'

"So the catcher thinks for a while and comes up with a plan. 'Gimmie the ball now,' he says, 'and I'll hide it under my chest protector. Then I'll go back to home plate and you pretend to throw the ball, like always. I'll whack the ball into my glove like I just caught it, and we'll see what the ump says.'

"So that's what they do. Feigner fakes throwing the pitch, the catcher fakes catching it, and the ump yells, 'Stee-rike! Yer outta here!'

"And all of a sudden, all hell breaks loose at home plate. The batter is screaming at the ump and kicking dirt on his shoes and the ump is pushing him with his chest and they're both gesturing with their hands and getting red in the face. The catcher wants nothing to do with any of that, so he walks away and goes back out to the pitching mound.

"'What's going on?' says Feigner.

"'Ah, you know,' says the catcher. 'Same old, same old. The batter thinks it was low and outside.'"

I laughed. "Cute, Unc, but what's the point?"

"It's not done yet, okay?"

"Sorry."

"So a year or so later, they're playing the same team again, and the same batter comes up in the bottom of the ninth. This time Feigner's arm is fine, but he throws the guy four balls, walks him. So the catcher goes out to the mound.

"'What the hell are you doing?' he says.

"'Paying for my sins,' says Feigner.

"'Yeah? Gee, Eddie, that's really nice. That's a fine thing to do.'

"'Thank you,' says Eddie.

"'You're welcome. Don't do it anymore.'

"And he didn't."

And neither did I.

Author's Notes

Minnesotans will be quick to note that I have taken some liberties with both time and place settings. Most of the Saint Paul settings are real, including the abandoned tunnel under Kellogg Park, but anybody trying to locate Lefty's Pool Hall or Nickel Pete's pawnshop will find himself on a fool's errand. The Ramsey County Jail moved from its location on the Mississippi River bluff several years ago, but in Herman Jackson's world, it is still there and always will be. It lets him keep his office downtown. The Iron Range is largely the way it was fifteen years ago, when I used to spend a fair amount of time there. Today, there is almost no trace of the original town of Mountain Iron. The bus station in Eveleth is a real historic reference, though it, too, is now gone. I got off at that station once in May, and the piles of plowed snow were still higher than the parked cars. The VFW bar is pure fabrication.

With history, I have been more scrupulous. The events that triggered the 1967 race riots in Detroit are well documented, and I have not altered them. My scenes in Vietnam are largely composites of the many stories told to me over the years by coworkers or classmates who were there.

The characters, of course, are another matter. If they bear any resemblance to anyone living or dead, it is a matter of pure coincidence, and nobody would be more astonished to discover it than I.

To receive a free catalog of Poisoned Pen Press titles, please contact us in one of the following ways:

Phone: 1-800-421-3976
Facsimile: 1-480-949-1707
Email: info@poisonedpenpress.com
Website: www.poisonedpenpress.com

Poisoned Pen Press
6962 E. First Ave. Ste. 103
Scottsdale, AZ 85251